PRAISE FO. P9-DEL-585

❤

"A NOVELIST WHO CAN'T WRITE THEM FAST ENOUGH."

—San Antonio Express-News

❤

"AUTHOR SANDRA BROWN PROVES HERSELF TOP-NOTCH."

—Associated Press

❤

"MILLIONS OF READERS CLAMOR FOR THE COMPELLING CONTEMPORARY NOVELS OF SANDRA BROWN. AND NO WONDER! She fires your imagination with irresistible characters, unexpected plot twists, scandalous secrets . . . tension so electric you feel the zing."

—The Literary Guild®

❤

"A MASTER STORYTELLER."

—Newport Daily News Press

❤

"ONE OF OUR TIME'S MOST TALENTED AUTHORS OF WOMEN'S FICTION."

—Affaire de Coeur

❤

"[A WRITER WHO] DEMONSTRATES HER MASTERY OF THE ROMANTIC SUSPENSE GENRE."

—Publishers Weekly

❤

"A GIFTED STORYTELLER."

—Rendezvous

❤

Dear Reader,

For years before I began writing general fiction, I wrote genre romances under several pseudonyms. *Prime Time* was originally published more than ten years ago (under my first pen name, Rachel Ryan).

This story reflects the trends and attitudes that were popular at that time, but its themes are eternal and universal. As in all romance fiction, the plot revolves around star-crossed lovers. There are moments of passion, anguish, and tenderness—all integral facets of falling in love.

I very much enjoyed writing romances. They're optimaistic in orientation and have a charm unique to any other form of fiction. If this is your first taste of it, please enjoy.

Sandra Brown

SANDRA BROWN

PRIME TIME

WARNER
VISION
BOOKS

A Time Warner Company

WARNER BOOKS EDITION

Copyright © 1983 by Sandra Brown
All rights reserved.

Cover design by Jackie Merri Meyer
Hand lettering by Carl Dellacroce
Cover photograph by Herman Estevez

This Warner Books Edition is published by arrangement with the author.

Warner Vision is a trademark of Warner Books, Inc.

Warner Books, Inc
1271 Avenue of the Americas
New York, NY 10020

 A Time Warner Company

Printed in the United States of America
First Warner Books Printing: September, 1995

10 9 8 7 6 5 4 3 2 1

Chapter One

❧

Are you sure he'll be here today?" Andy Malone asked impatiently and shifted her weight into a more comfortable position. The "padded" stool in front of the counter was inaptly named—what padding there was beneath the red vinyl was lumpy and hard.

"Nope, sure ain't," Gabe Sanders, proprietor and chief cook of Gabe's Chili Parlor, said as he ran an unbleached muslin towel around the rim of a clean, but cracked and stained coffee mug. "All I said was that he was *likely* to be in today. That don't necessarily make it so, ya see? He's likely to do just what he damn well pleases." The grizzled old man chuckled.

Andy's trained instincts twitched with renewed anticipation, and she forgot the hard, uneven surface of the barstool she was sitting on. She knew better than to attract the attention of the other lunchtime customers or to show too much interest in her quarry. At any moment Gabe Sanders might decide she was a nosy outsider and stop answering her questions altogether.

"Oh?" She took a nonchalant sip of iced tea. It had been served to her in a red plastic glass with the teaspoon standing upright in it. "Does Mr. Ratliff strike you as an impulsive person?"

The moment it was out, she knew the question had put Gabe on his guard. The towel stopped trying to polish the hopelessly stained coffee mug. Gabe's bushy eyebrows dropped low over shrewd, now perceptibly less friendly eyes. "Just why're you asking so many questions about Lyon Ratliff? Huh?"

Quickly composing a cover story, Andy leaned forward in what she hoped was a confidence-inspiring pose and said conspiratorially, "I had a classmate at SMU who came from here. She told me about this man who lived on a big ranch and drove a silver El Dorado. I thought he sounded like someone out of a movie."

Gabe eyed her speculatively, and her self-assurance seemed to seep out of her slowly as his eyes peeled away her facade. His look frankly told her she looked too old to be a college student and that that was just one of her fibs. "Who was she?"

Completely disconcerted, first by Gabe's intuitive appraisal of her and now by his question, she stammered, "Who was . . . who?"

"Who was that classmate of yours? I probably know her. Been serving chili and burgers here since '47. Know most the families in Kerrville."

"Oh, well then you wouldn't know ... uh ... Carla. Actually she grew up in San Antonio and only came here in the summers to visit cousins or something." Andy reached for the glass of tea and took a deep swallow as though it had a restorative tonic in it.

Ever since arriving in this community in the Texas hill country a few days ago, she had felt like a fish out of water. The careful, polite inquiries that usually got her through doors that remained closed to anyone else, had gotten her nowhere. It was as though the citizenry of Kerrville were protecting Lyon Ratliff and her ultimate target, his reclusive father.

General Michael Ratliff was the last surviving five-star general of World War II. Andy had vowed to interview him for her television program. And if the sketchy news reports of his failing health were true, it would have to be soon. So far, her trip had produced not even a flicker of hope that she would accomplish that feat. Now Gabe Sanders was being as reticent and stingy with information as everyone else she had encountered.

Determination raised the chin of her heart-shaped face, but the corners of her mouth lifted into a sweet smile. Her sherry-colored eyes shone beguilingly. "Mr. Sanders, would you by any chance have a slice of lime for my tea?" Her self-confidence returned when Gabe seemed momentarily flustered by the radiance of her smile.

"How 'bout lemon? Will that do?"

"Wonderful! Thank you."

She pushed back a strand of golden-brown hair. She used her attractiveness to wheedle out information only when she was forced to, and it always galled her. She'd rather be able to tackle a story with the same forthrightness granted a male reporter simply by virtue of his sex. But when necessary, she wasn't averse to using any advantage, and if someone found her extraordinary coloring intriguing, there was no harm in being cordial. Her father, who had had a poetic flair, had once compared her to an ice cream parfait made with vanilla ice cream, Amaretto, and caramel sauce.

"Thank you," she said when Gabe returned with two lemon wedges on a saucer. She squeezed the juice of one into the glass of tea, which had been presweetened and tasted like syrup to her, since she rarely used sugar in anything.

"You're not from around here, are you?"

She was tempted to invent a lie in answer to Gabe's question, but suddenly the fun had gone out of the game. "No, I'm not. I live in Nashville now, though I grew up in Indiana."

"Nashville, huh? You with the Grand Ole Opry?"

She laughed, shaking her head. "No. I work for an independent cable company."

"Cable?" Gabe's eyebrows jumped, and Andy decided they were his most expressive feature. "Ya mean television-like cable?"

4

"Yes."

"Are you on TV?"

"Sometimes. I have an interview show that's syndicated to cable stations across the country."

"Interviews?" He looked beyond her shoulder and around the room at his other customers, as though looking for someone she might consider interviewing. Then his eyes swung back to her with sudden comprehension. "You wouldn't be thinkin' 'bout askin' Lyon for an interview with his daddy, now, would ya?"

"Yes. I am."

He studied her for a moment. "There wasn't any classmate at SMU, was there?"

She met his eyes steadily. "No."

"I didn't think so." There was no censure in his voice.

"Do you think Mr. Ratliff will refuse to let me interview his father?"

"Sure as hell do, but we're fixin' to find out, 'cause that's him a-comin' in now."

Andy's eyes dropped to the wet ring her glass had left on the counter top just as her stomach dropped to her feet. The cowbell that hung on the metal bar across the door clanged loudly as he pushed through it.

"Hey, Lyon," someone said from the corner of the diner.

"Lyon," another customer called out.

"Jim, Pete." His voice was deep and raspy. The sound rippled toward her, pricked the small of her back like a needle, and generated a shiver that feathered up her spine.

She had hoped he would take a stool on either side of her, so it would be easy to strike up a conversation. But the footsteps she tracked with her ears took him to the end of the bar, to an extension that ran perpendicular to the counter where she was seated. Out of the corner of her eye she saw a blue shirt. Gabe ambled toward it.

"Hiya, Lyon? What'll ya have? Chili?"

"Not today. It's too hot. Besides Gracie fixed chili the other night, and it took two doses of that pink gunk to get my stomach back in shape."

"Could that bellyache have had anything to do with the margaritas you were drinking with that chili?"

A low laugh rumbled out of what must surely be a massive chest. "Could've been, could've been." That voice. What kind of man had such a stirring voice? Andy didn't think her curiosity could hold out much longer. Surrendering at last, she looked at him just as he said, "Give me a cheeseburger basket."

"Comin' up."

Andy didn't even hear Gabe's reply to Lyon Ratliff's order. She was too taken with the man who had given it. He wasn't at all what she had expected. She had pictured him as older, well into middle age, probably because General Ratliff was in his eighties. Apparently his son had been born after the war. She estimated Lyon Ratliff's age at around thirty-five.

Thick, dark hair lay in sculpted strands around his head. It was threaded at the temples with silver. Two sleek, dark

6

brows arched over eyes whose color she couldn't determine from that distance. Her eyes followed the length of the Roman nose, which reminded her of actors who play in Biblical films, to the sensual mouth, which reminded her of actors who play in another type of film.

"Is that Ratliff beef you're frying up for me on that grill?" he asked Gabe.

Again Andy was intrigued by his voice. It was resonant, but quiet, as if you might miss something of great importance if you didn't listen very closely. The hoarse quality lent a sexy undertone to everything he said. Definitely more like the second type of actor than the first.

"You bet," Gabe said. "Best beef a body can buy."

Lyon's dark head tilted back slightly, and he chuckled. He was lowering his head and reaching for the glass of icewater Gabe had set before him when his eyes accidentally slid over her. Momentum earned them a few inches past her before they braked, reversed, and backed up slowly.

Andy could log the journey those gray eyes — yes, they were gray — took over her face. They started with her own eyes, and she read in his the expected surprise. It was the usual reaction of anyone who was looking into her eyes for the first time. They were a captivating tawny-brown, surrounded by thick, dark lashes.

The gray eyes lifted to her hair. Did the ponytail held in place on the nape of her neck by a tortoise shell clasp make her look too young? Or, God forbid, did she look like a thirty-year-old *trying* to look young?

Don't get paranoid, Andy, she warned herself. She knew her caramel-colored hair with its golden streaks was attractive. But the beads of perspiration along her hairline? Could he detect that? Even though Gabe's twenty-year-old sign in the window boasted Refrigerated Air Inside, Andy was aware of a sheen of perspiration glossing her entire body. Indeed, she was suddenly acutely aware of every pore of her body, every nerve. It was as though she had been slit open for dissection, and Lyon Ratliff was a scientist who was taking his time about examining this particular specimen.

When his eyes moved to her mouth, she looked away. She reached for her glass and almost let it slip through her fingers before taking a drink. Then she was afraid that rather than diverting his attention from her lips, she had only attracted more attention to them.

What was the matter with her? She had a job to do. For three days she had been stalking this man, asking leading questions about him and his father, gathering whatever crumbs of information were thrown to her, enduring rude dismissals. For hours she had sat in that tacky beauty salon and listened to all the local gossip, hoping for the mention of his name, and all the while refusing, kindly but firmly, to have her hair permed "just to give it body." The only thing she learned there was that Lyon had had to miss the last country club dance because his daddy had taken a turn for the worse, and that new plants had been ordered for his ranch house, and that the resident manicurist had been trained by the Marquis de Sade.

Now, here he was, sitting a few feet from her, and she was sweaty and tongue-tied for the first time in her life. Where was all her cool confidence? The sheer bull-headedness that always kept her from taking no for an answer had deserted her. The objectivity that distinguished her was swamped by sexual awareness of a man. She had met kings and prime ministers and presidents, including two presidents of the United States, and she hadn't been intimidated by one of them. *Now, this . . . this cowboy strolls into a greasy spoon of a diner, and I'm all aflutter.*

Stubbornly trying to restore her control, she raised her chin and looked at him defiantly. His eyes could have been twin boulders that rolled over her and crushed her bravery. His jaw was tilted at an arrogant angle. He could have spoken aloud, and she couldn't have gotten the message any clearer.

Yes, I've heard of the equality of the sexes, and I think it's fine in its way. But right now I'm looking at you and thinking of you only as a sex object, and there's not one damn thing you can do about it.

Well, there was *one* thing she could do. She could stop him from thinking what he was thinking. She'd inform him in a calm, professional manner who she was and why she was here . . . just as soon as he finished his cheeseburger, she decided, as Gabe set the heaping plate in front of him.

Andy studied Gabe's dusty-greasy menu, which had been updated through the years by ineffectually painting

9

over the old prices to paint on the new. She suffered another glass of the oversweetened tea. She watched as a mother wiped the catsup off her little boy's mouth, then watched as another red smear replaced the first one when a whole french fry disappeared into his mouth. She fidgeted with the wire rack in front of her that contained three varieties of steak sauce. She pulled four paper napkins from the dispenser and blotted up the puddle her tea glass seemed bent on replenishing.

Finally she glanced toward the end of the counter and saw that Lyon had eaten most of his meal. He was sipping a cup of coffee, his long, slender, strong-looking fingers wrapped possessively around the mug. His absorption with the midday traffic outside the wide windows ended just as she slipped off the high stool, and he looked at her. She smiled and wished it didn't feel like a girlish, flirtatious, wobbly facsimile of one.

"Hello," she said, managing to walk over, despite shaky knees, to stand beside his stool.

His eyes made a slow and thorough appraisal. He looked at her with barely suppressed amusement and an air of sexual assessment not even moderately suppressed. Was he that accustomed to strange women approaching him in cafés? "Hi."

So, he was going to make it difficult, give her no lead-ins. Okay, Mr. Ratliff. She took a deep breath and said, "I'm Andrea Malone."

Andy couldn't have guessed that his facial expression could change so rapidly and so drastically, or that the eyes beneath those dark brows could harden and freeze over so quickly. He stared coldly at her for a long time, then presented her with a back view of his broad shoulders as he turned away. As though she didn't exist, he insouciantly took a sip of his coffee.

She glanced at Gabe, who was ostensibly concentrating on filling a salt shaker but whose ears she imagined were peaked with avid listening. She moistened her lips with her tongue. "I said I'm—"

"I know who you are, Ms. Malone," he said with a condescending sneer. "You're from Nashville. Telex Cable Television Company."

"Then you read the return address even though you didn't deign to open my letters before sending them back. Is that right?" she asked, in what she hoped was a haughty challenge.

"That's right." He took another drink of coffee. His indifference was irritating. She had an intense desire to take the coffee mug from his hand—if that were physically possible—and hurl it across the room, just to get his attention. However, she predicted that such an impulse could result in bodily harm. He seemed to radiate a strength of body and will, and she didn't want to trifle with either if at all possible. She was stubborn, but she wasn't stupid. "Mr. Ratliff, you know—"

"I know what you want. The answer is no. I believe I told you that after receiving your first letter several months ago. That one I *did* answer. Obviously you don't remember the contents of that letter. It said, in essence, for you to save your breath, your strength, your time, your money, and"—he raked her with cynical eyes—"your new clothes. I'd never consent to letting you interview my father for that television program. My sentiments are the same today as they were then." Rudely he turned his back on her again.

She had thought her new jeans and western boots would blend into the local scenery. Was she that conspicuous? All right. She had made one blunder. Perhaps all her sneaking around the past few days had been unprofessional, but she wasn't going to give up now. She squared her shoulders, unknowingly stretching the western-cut cotton shirt over her breasts. "You haven't even listened to what I propose, Mr. Ratliff. I—"

"I don't want to hear it." His head swung around to her again and his eyes unintentionally encountered her breasts on a level that was disadvantageous to them both. She stood perfectly still, as though to move would admit to the untenability of the situation. After a considerable time he raised his eyes, and she caught her breath at the fierceness of his look.

"No interviews with my father," he said in a low, tense voice. "He's an old man. He doesn't feel well. Others, bigger and better than you, Ms. Malone, have come asking. The answer remains irrevocably no."

He pushed himself off the stool, and she realized when she found herself looking at his collarbone that he was very tall. She took a step back and watched with fascination as his hand dug into the pocket of his tight jeans to extract a five-dollar bill. The intrusion of his hand, pulling tighter the already taut denim, sent hot color rushing to her cheeks. He laid the bill down next to his plate. According to the grimy menu, it was more than twice what a cheeseburger basket cost.

"Thanks, Gabe. See ya."

"See ya, Lyon."

Andy couldn't believe she was being so blithely dismissed when he sidestepped her on his way to the front door. "Mr. Ratliff," she said on a grating note, following him.

He stopped and turned around with slow deliberation, much more menacing than if he'd whipped around quickly. She felt that she was being lacerated by tiny rapiers as his eyes sliced down her body from the top of her head to the toes of her shiny new boots.

"I don't like pushy broads, Ms. Malone. You impress me as such. I will not permit my father to be interviewed by anyone, especially by you. So why don't you pack up your new clothes and get your cute little butt back to Nashville where it belongs?"

She flung her purse on the bed and collapsed into the uncomfortable chair in the small, stuffy motel room. Eight fingers were pressed against her forehead while her thumbs rotated over her pounding temples. She didn't know if it was the heat, or the arid climate, or the man, but something had given her a whale of a headache. The man. No doubt it had been the man.

13

Standing up after a few minutes of rest, she pulled off her boots and kicked them aside. "Thanks for nothing." She went into the bathroom to swallow two aspirins with lukewarm water out of the cold-water tap.

"Why didn't you slap his smug face?" she asked her image in the mirror. "Why did you just stand there like a big dummy and take that abuse?" She released her hair from its clasp and shook it loose, a motion which did her headache no good. "Because you want that interview, that's why."

She dreaded calling Les. What would she tell him? He didn't take disappointment well, and that was putting it mildly. Possibilities of what she would say were still bouncing around in her mind when she dialed the long-distance number. She called collect and person-to-person, and after being channeled through the switchboard operator at Telex to Les's office, she heard his querulous growl. "Yeah?"

"Hi, it's me."

"Well, well, I was beginning to think you'd been taken hostage by cattle rustlers or something. It was nice of you to take the time to call."

Sarcasm. Today's mood was sarcasm. Andy accepted it with resignation, as she accepted all Les's moods. "I'm sorry, Les, but I didn't have anything to report, so I didn't call. Remember your memo last month about unnecessary long-distance calls?"

"But that doesn't apply to you, Andy baby," he said more cordially. "How's it going down there in cow country?"

14

She rubbed her forehead as she answered. "Not too well. I got nowhere for the first few days. All I found out for certain was that there was some landscaping being done at the ranch house. That's it. That, and where Lyon Ratliff, the son, sometimes eats lunch when he comes into town. Today I had the pleasure of meeting the gentleman."

She stared at her nylon-covered toes, remembering not the hateful way he had spoken to her before he stalked out the door, but the way he'd looked at her the first time their eyes had met. She hadn't felt that way in the presence of a man since . . . she'd *never* felt that way in the presence of a man.

"And?" Les prodded impatiently.

"Oh . . . and . . . uh . . . it's going to be tough, Les. He's as hardheaded as a mule. Impossible to talk to. Stubborn, rude, insulting."

"Sounds like a real nice guy." Les laughed.

"He was bloody awful." She toyed with a string on the Spanish-red and black bedspread. "I don't feel right about this anymore, Les. Maybe we shouldn't be forcing the issue. What if the old general really is too ill to be interviewed? The reports on his health may be inaccurate. It's possible he's incapable of withstanding the strain of a series of interviews. He may not even be able to talk. What would you say to my giving up this one and coming home?"

"Andy baby, what's happening to you out there? That Texas sun baking your brain?"

She could just see Les now. He'd lower his Hush Puppy-shod feet from the desk and bring his chair forward to prop his elbows on the littered desk in his "earnest" pose. The horn-rimmed glasses would either be shoved to the top of his head to perch on his red hair or would be taken off altogether and set down amidst the overflowing ashtrays and empty candy wrappers and week-old scripts. If she were there rather than a thousand miles away, she would become the victim of startling cold blue eyes. Even through the telephone wire she could feel those eyes boring into her.

"You aren't going to let a bad-tempered bully stand in your way, are you? Baby, you've come up against worse. Much worse. Remember those union goons in that picket line? They threatened our photographer with billy clubs, yet you had them eating out of your hand in ten minutes. Course, they were all hot for your body. But then so is any man with—"

"Les," she said tiredly. "Please."

"Please what? I'd like to hear you say, 'Please, Les.' Anytime."

She and Les Trapper and Robert Malone had begun their careers together at a small television station. Les had produced news shows. Robert had been a reporter. Andy had co-anchored the evening news broadcasts with a myopic dolt who had been with the television station since its inception and whom the management didn't have the heart to fire.

Even after she and Robert had gotten married, the friendship among the three of them remained inviolate. When Robert was hired as a correspondent for the

16

network, he was away from home much of the time. Les had helped relieve the lonely hours, but always as a friend only.

She remembered vividly the night Les came to her house and told her that Robert had been killed in Guatemala, where he had been covering an earthquake. Les had cushioned her for weeks, taking over responsibilities that were too grim for her to handle. For months after Robert's death she had used him as a shield between her and the rest of the world. He relished the role of protector.

Since then they had continued to be friends and worked together now for Telex. She knew better than to take his ribald suggestions seriously. Les was never, nor ever had been, without a woman, or *women*.

His only real love was his work and always had been and always would be. He was ambitious to a fault. He wasn't above doing anything to get a story. He was shrewd and, more often than Andy wanted to admit, lacking in sensitivity. His language was foul, his moods unpredictable.

But he was still her friend. And her supervisor. And she'd better come up with something fast.

"What if I got Lyon Ratliff to consent to an interview? He would be—"

"Dull as hell. Wouldn't tell us a damn thing. And who the hell cares about him? We need the old man, Andy. And we need him now before he kicks off. You still want to go to network, don't you?"

"Yes, of course. More than anything."

"Okay, so stop this pussyfooting around." His tone softened appreciably. "Andy baby, you could knock the big boys and girls at network right on their fat cushy cans. You've got the talent. You're the best interviewer in the country. You made a mass murderer cry. I saw it, and I wasn't even wearing my glasses. You're younger, smarter, sexy as hell with those damn gold eyes and that luscious body of yours. Put them to work. Seduce this cowboy and—"

"Les!"

"Oh, yeah, I nearly forgot. I'm speaking to the most frigid female ever created to curse man. Look, Andy, who're you saving it for? I sure as hell know it isn't for me, and it's not for lack of trying. Ever since Robert got killed you've lived the life of a vestal virgin. For three years for God's sakes. Loosen up a bit, baby. Bat those long lashes at that cowpoke, and he'll be putty in your hands."

She almost wanted to laugh at the absurdity of Lyon Ratliff's ever being putty in anyone's hands. Instead she sighed wearily. To a degree Les was right. She had no life outside her work. Perhaps it was because Robert had been killed while on assignment. Perhaps it was because her father had been a noted journalist. Andy Malone felt compelled to succeed in broadcast journalism.

Working at Telex wasn't her idea of the top of the ladder, though she had nationwide visibility. She wanted to work for a network. To land a job like that, she needed to pull off a coup. An interview with General Michael Ratliff would be guaranteed to get the attention of a network executive.

"All right, Les. I don't agree with your means, but I do want the same ends. I'll give it another shot."

"That's my girl. How about the landscaping angle? Think you could pass yourself off as a pituitary?"

"That's a gland, you idiot, not a shrub. I think you mean pyracantha or pittosporum."

"Hell. I never could keep my glands straight. I only knew what to do with them."

"Good-bye, Les."

"Good-bye. I love ya."

"Love you, too. Good-bye."

She spent the rest of the afternoon lying on a chaise beside the motel pool, feeling as though she had earned a half-day off. Her brain and insides felt battered, though no visible signs of injury showed on her body in the skimpy bikini that elicited whistles from three teenage boys driving by in a pickup truck. Their flirting was harmless.

Lyon Ratliff's was not.

It had been hours since she had come under the careful perusal of his eyes, but her body responded to the recollection so strongly that it could be happening again. Her breasts tingled with sensations she had thought long dead; her nipples were prominent beneath the cloth of her bikini bra. A heaviness like a giant heart had settled in the lower part of her body. At regular intervals it pulsed, suffusing her with life and reminding her that she hadn't died in that earthquake with Robert.

She drove her rented compact car to a carry-out barbecue restaurant and brought a juicy sandwich back to her room. Later she tried to watch television, but became bored with the inane sitcoms and variety shows. She tried to read the latest sizzling novel. Though the hero had been described as blond and green-eyed, she could only envision dark unruly hair and gray eyes. A sensual, insolent mouth that could harden in anger but which promised unforgettable kisses. A tall, lean body that made one resent clothes. A ruggedly handsome, suntanned face that defined virility. The hero of the book paled by comparison.

"He's the rudest man I've ever met," she said as she tossed the novel aside and went to check the chain lock on the door. Before she snapped off the bedside lamp, she cast a furtive glance over her shoulder at the image reflected in the dresser mirror. She was wearing a T-shirt and sheer bikini panties. "But he's not all wrong," she said confidently and snapped off the light. It *was* cute.

She couldn't believe it had been so easy! All she remembered overhearing in the beauty salon was that Lyon Ratliff had ordered some plants from a nursery for supplementary landscaping. The nursery owner's wife had proudly announced to everyone that her husband was to deliver and plant them on Thursday morning.

Andy had awakened that morning with the plan already formed in her mind. Silently she thanked Les for the inspiration. She had dressed professionally in a summer-weight suit of raw silk with a sleeveless coral silk blouse underneath. She twisted her hair into a bun on the back of her neck in a style that radiated competence. She drove her car to within a mile of the Ratliff ranch and pulled it off the highway, hoping she wasn't too late.

She had sat on the side of the highway for twenty minutes before she saw the nursery truck lumbering down the highway with its load of plants. She had jumped out of her car, raised the hood, and stood looking helpless and distressed by the side of the road. As she had expected, the nursery truck ground to a halt on the shoulder just after passing her. She ran around its slated sides to the driver, who was climbing out of the cab.

"Thanks so much for stopping," she said breathlessly.

"Morning. What happened to your car, little lady?"

She gritted her teeth behind her false smile. "I don't know," she wailed piteously. "I was on my way to the Ratliff ranch. I was already late for an appointment with Gracie and now this! She's going to wonder what happened to me. Could you please give me a lift to the nearest telephone?"

She had no idea who Gracie was. She had only heard Lyon mention her in Gabe's restaurant. She could either be a relative, a cook, housekeeper . . . wife? Had she ever read that he was married? Why did it upset her to think he might be? In any event her ruse about the appointment with Gracie had worked. The nurseryman grinned broadly.

"I can do you one better than that. I'm going to the Ratliffs'. How'd you like a ride to the front door?"

Her hand had flown to her chest as though to still a rapidly beating heart. "You're not serious! Oh, you'd be a lifesaver. I can conduct my business and call about my car at the same time. Are you sure you don't mind?" she had asked, treating him to the full brilliance of her smile.

"Not atall, not atall."

"Just let me get my purse and lock the car." She had spun around on her bone pumps and trotted back to her car, thanking her stars that the man had been so easily duped. He hadn't even asked what her business was.

Modesty had to be sacrificed for her to climb into the truck, but Mr. Houghton, as he had introduced himself, was a perfect gentleman and turned his head.

The cab of the truck was noisy, dusty, and smelled of earth and fertilizer, but now Andy was chatting to Mr. Houghton inconsequentially as they pulled up to the electric security gate surrounding the Ratliff ranch.

The brakes wheezed as Mr. Houghton stepped on the pedal, but apparently Lyon had notified the guard of the arrival of the nursery truck. The gates swung wide on the blacktopped road, and they were waved through by a toothless guard wearing a cowboy hat. If he saw Andy or noted that she didn't look like a gardener, he didn't do anything about it. She breathed a huge sigh of relief as the truck rolled through the gate and she saw through the mirror mounted outside her window that it was closing behind them.

"I'll just let you out at the front. I'm supposed to meet Mr. Ratliff around on the west side."

"That will be wonderful," she said, smiling. More wonderful than she had anticipated. Lyon would be busy for a while. *Lyon?* Had she thought simply "Lyon"?

The house was awesome and looked like it belonged in Southern California instead of on the Texas plains. Nestled in a grove of pecan, oak, and cottonwood, its sprawling proportions were redeemed by a certain grandeur. It was a two-story house, but this didn't prevent her from getting the impression that its various wings seemingly stretched for acres.

The house itself and all the outbuildings were of white adobe and roofed with burnt-red tile. Four arches across the front of the house supported the wide, deep front porch where hanging baskets boasted ferns, petunias, begonia, and impatiens. The colors were vibrant. The shade was deep, and the white of the house was pristine and glaring by contrast.

"Thank you again, Mr. Houghton," she said as he pulled to a grinding stop and then maneuvered the gearshift back into first.

"You're quite welcome, little lady. I hope there's nothing seriously wrong with your car."

"I do too." She jumped down from the cab, jarring both her teeth and the chignon on the back of her neck. She shut the door softly, so as not to attract attention, and was gratified when it closed with only a minimum of racket. Taking slow, careful steps, she stopped ostensibly to admire a basket of flowers. When the truck had rounded the side of the house, she stepped into the shadows of the front porch.

There was a wide window to correspond with each of the arches. Feeling like a criminal, she crept over to each one, cupped her hands against the panes of glass, and peered inside. The rooms had high ceilings, were well furnished and immaculately clean. There was a living room with an enormous fireplace and comfortable sofas and chairs, a study with bookcase-lined walls and a massive desk littered with papers, and a dining room. The last room had a terrazzo tile floor and wicker furniture. Through the window Andy could see that one of the side walls was solid glass. The room was filled with tropical plants. A ceiling fan circled overhead.

An old man was sitting in a wheelchair, reading—or was he sleeping? She went around the corner of the house to the other side and looked through the sliding glass door. He was reading. A book lay in his lap. His age-spotted hand turned the page slowly. A pair of wire-rimmed eyeglasses were mounted on his bony nose.

Andy jumped when, without even looking up at her, he said, "Come in, Mrs. Malone."

Chapter Two

❧

Shock paralyzed her. She couldn't have said which surprised her the most, that the old man had known she was there in the first place or his benign expression as he looked up at her and smiled. She was as surprised by the father as she had been by the son. She had expected something like George C. Scott's portrayal of General Patton. Where was the stern military bearing? The General Michael Ratliff of today exemplified benevolence. She had seen pictures of him, but they had been taken forty years ago and bore little resemblance to the frail old man in the wheelchair.

Her incredulity seemed to amuse him. "Come in closer where I can see you better, please, Mrs. Malone."

Andy forced her legs to propel her through the opened glass door and, into the garden room. "Are you General Ratliff?" she asked hesitantly.

He chuckled. "Of course."

"H—" she swallowed hard. "How do you know who I am? Were you expecting me?" She wondered briefly if Les had called to ask the general for an interview but dismissed the idea before it was full-blown. That wasn't exactly Les's technique. And besides that, no one talked to the general without first consulting Lyon. Lyon's mind wouldn't easily be changed.

"Yes, I was expecting you," he said, with no further word of explanation. "Please sit down. Would you care for something to drink?"

"No, no, thank you." Why did she suddenly feel like a school girl caught out in a mischievous prank? She sat on the edge of one of the wicker chairs with a high, fanned back and a bold print cushion. She tucked her envelope purse between her thigh and the armrest and tugged at the hemline of her skirt. Her back was erect. "You didn't look up before speaking to me. How—"

"Military training, Mrs. Malone. I've always had ears like radar. My excellent hearing was the bane of my junior officers. They never could criticize me without my hearing them." He chuckled again.

"But how did you know my name?" In spite of having been caught red-handed spying and trespassing, she was enjoying herself. It was a heady feeling to know she was at last in the presence of one of her country's most illustrious war heroes. He was feeble of body, but his mind was razor-sharp. His eyes were rheumy, but she suspected that they saw more than he wanted people to know. Or was it his keen perception that made it seem that way? His sparse white hair was neatly combed, military fashion. He was dressed in an impeccably starched and ironed one-piece jumpsuit. "Have you ever seen my television program?" she asked him.

"No, I regret to say that I have not. I knew who you were because Lyon told me that he had met you in town yesterday." He watched for her reaction.

She smoothed her features into a placid mask. "Oh?" she asked coolly. "Did he also tell you how rudely he behaved?"

The old man laughed a loud, short, barking laugh that set off a fit of coughing. She jumped up, alarmed, and leaned over him, ready to help. She had no idea what to do and didn't even want to consider the repercussions should anything happen to him while they were alone. The spasm finally subsided, and he waved her back into her chair. After taking several deep breaths he said, "No, Lyon failed to mention his rudeness, but it sounds like him."

He wiped his streaming eyes with a white linen handkerchief. When he was done, Andy could have sworn there was mischief lurking in them. "He told me that another leech from the press was nosing around town asking questions. He called you . . . let's see . . . a nosy bitch. Yes, I think those were his exact words. He went on to

27

say that no doubt you thought you could use your face and body to get a story out of a corpse. Then he described you in great detail."

Hot color flooded her cheeks, and she gnashed her teeth in anger. That wretch! *Leech. Bitch.* And to think he'd accuse her of something so despicable.

She wanted to wallow in her anger, to savor it, but realized that the general was weighing her reaction to his son's account of their meeting with interest. "General Ratliff, I want you to know that your son is wrong about me. True, I was asking questions about you and your life here at the ranch, but only because I want—"

"You don't have to defend yourself to me, Mrs. Malone. I'm only telling you how you impressed Lyon. So that I may form my own unbiased opinion, let me get the facts straight. You work for a cable network, and you want to interview me for your television program. Is that correct?"

"Yes, sir. We, that is *I*, want to do a series of interviews that could be run on consecutive nights for a week. The programs would be a half-hour each."

"Why?"

"Why?" she echoed, not understanding his question.

"Why do you want to interview me?"

She stared at him in perplexity, shook her head slightly and said, "General Ratliff, surely you can guess that. You're a part of American history. Your name will be in every textbook written about World War II. For years you've kept yourself sequestered on this ranch. The

American public is curious to know why. They want to know what you're doing."

"I can answer that in one word: nothing. I sit here day after day, getting older, deteriorating, waiting to die." He held his palm up when he saw her about to protest. "Now, Mrs. Malone, if we're ever going to work together, we must be honest with each other. I am about to die. I've waited a long time for it, and I'm rather looking forward to it. I'm tired of being old and useless."

There was nothing for her to say, so she kept silent as they stared at each other. It was the general who spoke first. "Hypothetically let's say that I agree to let you interview me. Could I lay down the terms of my capitulation, so to speak?"

Her heart began to pound. He was going to agree. "Yes, sir."

"Very well. You may have your interviews, Mrs. Malone, though why you would rather interview me than some much more dashing figure is beyond me."

"I think you're quite dashing," she said and meant it.

He laughed, much less violently this time. "In my youth perhaps. Now, as to my terms. You may ask anything about my childhood, my schooling, my military training, my career before and since the war. I was a foot soldier in World War I. Did you know that?" Without waiting for an answer, he continued. "You may question me about the war as a whole, but I will not discuss individual battles."

"Very well," she said slowly.

"I will be quite blunt in refusing to answer should you ask a question about a specific battle."

"I understand." She didn't, but she'd agree to anything at this point just for the chance to get the interviews.

"When do we start? Today?"

She grinned at his enthusiasm. "No. I'll notify my crew tonight, and they'll arrive with the equipment in a day or so."

"Will the interviews be on film?"

"Video tape."

"Video tape," he said musingly, as though he couldn't quite grasp the concept.

"It does the same thing as film, but doesn't have to be processed. It's like tape in an audio tape recorder, except with the video, too." He nodded solemnly. "I can use the time until the crew gets here to select settings. I don't want all the interviews to be recorded in the same place."

"And we'll have a chance to get to know one another," he said, winking at her. "How long will it take?"

"We'll work every day only as long as you feel well. I think if we recorded one complete program a day, that would be acceptable to everyone. We should be finished—"

"You're already finished."

The harsh words burst into the room from the doorway through which Andy had come in. She whipped her head around to see Lyon as a menacing silhouette against the bright landscape outside. His hands were planted on his hips. He was dressed in jeans, a western shirt, and dusty cowboy boots. His hair was windblown. His expression was ferocious.

"Come in, Lyon. I believe you already know our guest, Mrs. Malone."

Lyon strode into the room. He pointedly ignored his father's attempted courtesy. Instead he glared at Andy. "What in the hell are you doing here?"

Andy sprang to her feet. She wasn't about to look up at him like a penitent. "You know what I'm doing here."

"I also know the underhanded way you managed to get through the gate. Mr. Houghton and I were well into the second row of boxwoods when he happened to mention the poor little lady he'd driven here to keep her appointment with Gracie after her car broke down. Gracie's been here longer than I have, and to my knowledge she's never had an 'appointment.' I put two and two together, and unfortunately it added up to you. Now, Ms. Malone, you're leaving. By force if necessary." She had no doubt that he meant it. He was reaching for her arm when his father deterred him.

"Lyon, your mother would be distressed by your lack of manners, especially toward a lady. I have consented to Mrs. Malone's interviewing me."

Had he been struck with a shovel, Lyon couldn't have looked more stunned. "Dad . . . you . . . are you sure?" Showing a sensitivity she wouldn't have thought him capable of, he knelt beside his father's wheelchair and placed his large, tanned hand on General Ratliff's shoulder. "Are you sure?" he repeated.

The general's eyes locked with his son's. "Yes, I'm sure. I won't do any others, but Mrs. Malone is so charming, I find I can't refuse her request."

"Charming be damned," Lyon snapped, rising to his feet. "Don't let her talk you into anything you don't want to do."

"Have you ever known me to be so gullible, Lyon?" he asked softly. "Don't worry. It'll be fine. I want to do this."

"Very well." Lyon's nod was equally terse.

"Well, Mrs. Malone, it seems that it's all settled," the general said pleasantly.

"Thank you, General Ratliff," she said, "but please call me Andy."

"I like you, Andy."

"I like you, too." She laughed and the general joined her, sharing the enjoyment of having met each other.

"Excuse me," Lyon said chillingly, driving a wedge of hostility into the congenial atmosphere, "but I have to get back to work."

"Lyon, let Mr. Houghton do what he knows to do. You take Andy back to wherever she's staying and help her move her things here."

Andy and Lyon turned in unison to face General Ratliff. Both stared at him in mute bewilderment. At long last Andy found her voice and stammered, "B—but I'm at the Haven in the Hills, and I assure you I'm quite comfortable."

"But not as comfortable as you'll be here," the general said amiably. "You've not tasted Gracie's cooking." *So,* thought Andy, *Gracie is the cook*. "And I may get the urge to bare my soul at any time of the day or night. You wouldn't want to risk missing that. All things considered, it'll be much better for you to stay under this roof until we are done with the project."

"But my crew will be at the motel and—"

"How many crewmen will there be?"

She tabulated quickly. "Four."

"Then we'll put them in the bunkhouse. There's plenty of room. I'll hear no more objections," he said, in a voice that was reminiscent of his former command. "Lyon and I are too much alone out here. You'll be a welcome diversion." He started the battery-operated motor of his chair. "Now, please excuse me. The two of you have tired me out. I'll see you at lunch."

The softly purring motor on the chair propelled it out of the room, and Andy was left alone with Lyon. He must have known of his father's auditory capabilities, for he waited until the wheelchair was out of sight before he turned to her. "You should be very proud of yourself."

She defied the accusation in the hard grey eyes. "I am. Your father readily agreed to the interviews. You could have saved us both a lot of time and trouble if you'd conveyed my request to him months ago rather than returning all my letters unopened."

"He may have consented to these interviews, but I haven't." He toured her with scornful eyes. "Isn't your life exciting enough? What motivates someone to pry into the personal lives of other people? Is that how you get your kicks?"

She hated the taunting curl of his mouth. "I'm not *prying*. I only want to talk to your father and record those conversations on tape, to be shared with thousands of people who will be interested in what he has to say."

"That sounds real good, Ms. Malone. Noble and forthright. You may very well be nominated for sainthood." The mocking smile was wiped from his face as if it had been swept away by a magic wand. His lips thinned to a resolute line. With violent speed he grasped her arm above the elbow and hauled her against him. The rigid lips barely moved as he said, "But I'm warning you, you do anything, *anything* to distress or harm my father, and you'll wish to God you hadn't. Do we have an understanding?"

The breath had been knocked out of her when her breasts had been flattened against the rock wall of his chest, but she struggled to get the words out. "We do."

He stared down at her, nodding his head slightly as if to say that he'd decide to believe her when she had proved herself. For moments that stretched into a small eternity he continued to stare at her. She couldn't breathe. Didn't dare. If she moved at all, she'd only call attention to the juxtaposition of their bodies, which suggested either a wrestling hold or a lovers' clinch, and either way she didn't want to acknowledge it.

At the same time she decided to remain perfectly still and not fight him, realization of their tempting proximity

34

dawned on his face. She was freed—suddenly, reflex-ively, instantly. An objective observer might have thought he considered being close to her dangerous. "Let's go get your things." The suggestion was no more than a growl. "I'm not a taxi service."

She wanted to come back with a scathing refusal, but she would have been speaking to his retreating back as it went through the glass door. She followed him around the length of the porch, which she learned surrounded the house, to the back, where his El Dorado was parked in a four-car garage.

He didn't even hold her door for her but went straight to the driver's side and slid behind the wheel. He had al-ready started the motor and was wearing an impatient, put-out look by the time she caught up with him and got in on the passenger side. She telegraphed what she thought of his manners by slamming the door hard. His reply came back clearly in the form of a stony silence. He didn't care what she thought.

They roared out the gate and down the highway. The scenery along the roadside blurred, and she didn't even want to guess how fast they were going. He drove with one elbow propped on the open window ledge and with his fingers tapping the roof of the car in time to a tune known only to him. The wind wreaked havoc with her hair, but she'd be damned if she'd ask him to close the window.

"That was my car," she said as they shot past the com-pact still parked on the shoulder of the opposing lane.

"We'll stop and get it on the way back. I wouldn't want anything to happen to the little lady."

She treated him to a murderous look before turning her head to stare out the window. It was her fervent wish that she could keep her motion sickness at bay as she watched the landscape roll by with sickening speed.

They didn't speak again until he braked the car within feet of the motel room door that bore the number matching the one on her key. She looked at him quizzically.

"You're not the only one who can ask nosy questions, Ms. Malone."

The gray eyes he leveled at her made her unaccountably nervous. What else had his inquiries about Andy Malone produced? "I'll be right back," she said, fumbling for the door handle and pushing her way out of the car. Even with the windows down, she'd found the confined space stifling.

Hurriedly unlocking her door, she went into her room. When the door wouldn't close behind her, she turned to see Lyon standing in the doorway with his hand splayed wide, holding it open. "I'll help."

"That isn't necessary."

"I didn't say it was."

Forcing her backward, he pushed his way inside and closed the door behind him. The room, which had seemed small before, shrunk to doll house proportions once he was inside. He tossed his car keys onto the middle of the bed, which the maid had already made up, then plopped down on it himself and leaned against the

36

headboard, stretching out his long legs so that his booted feet barely hung over the edge. When Andy just stood in the middle of the room staring at him, he said, "Don't let me bother you." His grin was arrogant and infuriating. It told her that he knew very well he was bothering her.

She turned her back on him and opened the suitcase lying on the rack in the closet alcove. She began furiously tearing garments from the hangers and stuffing them haphazardly into the suitcase. Several pairs of shoes were picked up from the floor and virtually thrown into her shoe bag. The drawstring popped and vibrated like a rubber band when she yanked it closed.

"Don't forget your boots," he said from the bed.

She whirled around. "I wouldn't dream of it. They go in a separate box. Thank you ever so much for your help."

He wasn't at all perturbed by her carefully enunciated sarcastic words. "Glad to oblige."

He smiled, and for a moment Andy was spellbound by a fantasy that was projected on her mind: Lyon leaning against the headboard of a bed and smiling at her, not with derision, but with intimacy. A strange tightness compressed her throat and forced all feeling downward to ripple across her abdomen. This sensation terrified her, and she fought vainly to stifle it.

She attacked the dressing table, heedlessly tossing her cosmetics and toiletries into her smaller suitcase. Bottles and jars rattled together, and she only hoped something wouldn't break and spill and ruin everything else. She glanced in the mirror over the basin and saw that Lyon's eyes hadn't wavered. He was watching each move.

"Do you take some prurient pleasure in watching this?"

"In fact I do. In my former life I must have been a peeping tom."

"You ought to work that out in analysis."

"Why?" His brows arched in curiosity. "Does my watching you make you nervous?"

"Not at all." The sardonic lift to the corner of his mouth told her that he knew she was lying. She dropped her eyes from his reflection in the mirror and crammed one last item into the carrying case.

Her hands faltered when she turned to the drawers in the dresser. It was stationed directly opposite the bed. Hastily she gathered slippery lingerie that wouldn't be grasped by her rushing fingers. She dropped a half-slip with a wide border of lace down each side. She retrieved it quickly, but not before a swift covert look in his direction informed her he had seen it. His smile was lewd with implications.

While she was stacking her notes that were lying helter-skelter on the small table and placing them in her brief-case, he heaved himself off the bed and sauntered into the bathroom. In a matter of seconds he came out carrying a raspberry-colored brassiere and panties set. She just now remembered that she'd rinsed them out the night before and hung them on the curtain rod to dry.

He carried a piece in each hand, never taking his eyes off her as he walked to within inches of her. His eyes held her pinned to the matted shag carpet. "Don't forget these," he drawled. Looking down at the sheer wisps in each of his hands, he assessed them with clinical accuracy. He tested their lightness by bouncing them and letting them float back into his palms. Entranced, she too stared at the garments. Through the glossy fabric she could read each line in his palm with the clarity of a fortune teller. "Not that they'd be missed that much. There's so little to them."

She gasped and snatched the bra and panties from his hands. He laughed as she threw them into the suitcase and slammed it shut. She lifted it off the rack, but he surprised her by coming to take it from her hand.

"Do you need to check out?" he asked, opening the door to the room.

"Yes," she said coldly, not wanting him to know that her heart was still beating so rapidly that her chest hurt.

"Then I'll load all this while you take care of that. I'll meet you at the office."

That was too convenient to argue with. "All right." She left the room and wended her way along the outdoor corridor until she reached the office. It took an interminable amount of time for the gum-popping clerk to sort out the paperwork, which, was aggravatingly complex for three nights' stay in a motel. As the clerk was running Andy's credit card through the machine she happened to see the El Dorado idling just beyond the door.

She eyed Andy speculatively. "That's Lyon Ratliff."

"Yes, it is," Andy said, staring at her in a way that dared her to ask any questions or make any comments.

"Hmmm" was all she said.

Andy left the office and slid into the passenger seat of the car. She liked the smell of the leather upholstery. She liked the way Lyon smelled, too. Even when he had come into the house from planting shrubbery, he had smelled of clean, musky male.

He had closed the window and turned on the air conditioner. Its hum was the only sound in the car until they reached the highway. Then he turned to her and asked, "What does Mr. Malone do while you're chasing all over the country invading other people's privacy?"

Stung by his insulting tone, she lashed out at him. "My husband is dead."

His face registered no emotion, but his eyes jerked back to the road. She looked away, too, wishing his profile weren't quite so appealing.

"I'm sorry," he said at last, quietly. "How did he die?"

His apology amazed her. His rapid changes of mood confused her. "He was killed while on assignment in Guatemala. The earthquake."

"How long ago?"

"Three years."

"He was a reporter?"

"Yes."

"Newspaper?"

"Television."

"He traveled a lot?"

"All the time. He was a stringer for one of the networks."

"Were you happy?"

Why the personal question? she wondered. The others he had asked had been those of a polite stranger trying to get acquainted. Her instinct was to tell him that her marital history was none of his business, but caution warned her not to. She would be asking his father questions. If she cooperated with Lyon's interrogation, maybe he would stop trying to sabotage the interviews with the general.

In addition to that she was weary of this game of one-upmanship, especially since she felt that in the long run he would win it. Could they call a truce?

"Yes, we were happy," she heard herself say.

He looked at her for a long time until she was tempted to take the wheel. He was still driving exceedingly fast. Finally he dragged his eyes back to the windshield.

Andy shifted in the glove-soft seat. There was a tension between them, an awareness, that made her throat ache. A compulsion to touch him overwhelmed her. She longed to know the texture of his thick, dark hair. The cloth of his shirt strained invitingly over the muscles defined beneath it. She wanted to squeeze the muscle of his thigh just to see if it were as hard as it looked under the denim of his jeans.

"How long have you done this type of work?"

His question pulled her back into a safer realm of thought. The air conditioner was doing little to cool the blood that raced through her veins. She cleared her throat. "Since I graduated from college. I started out writing copy for commercials at a local television station, graduated to the news department, then eventually became an anchorperson."

"But now you're more into the investigative side of things."

"Yes," she said hesitantly, justifiably wary of where this conversation might lead.

"I wonder why," he mused aloud. "You know, sometimes men who travel a lot choose that kind of work because they're unhappy at home. Is this some kind of guilt trip you've laid on yourself? You made your husband unhappy, so he went down to Central America and got himself killed, and now you're trying to make it up to him by following in his footsteps?"

He was so close to the truth that she felt she had been pierced by a spear of conscience and was dying a slow, agonizing death. But as with all wounded animals, she bristled with defiance. "How dare you say such a thing to me. You know nothing about Robert, about me. You—"

"I know all about you. You're an overbearing, over-ambitious female with an inflated ego because you happen to be better looking than most." He whipped the car off the road onto the shoulder and braked jarringly behind her car. She reached for the door handle, but his hand shot across her chest to trap her wrist in an iron grip. His face was close to hers as he bent over her. His voice was a harsh rasp.

"Don't think because you've got a beautiful face, and great legs, and breasts that dare a man to touch them that

42

I don't know you're as hard as nails. Your skin may be warm and soft, but you're a block of ice on the inside. I know your type well, Andy Malone. You'll castrate any man stupid enough to give you the chance. I'm not that stupid. So while you're doing these damn interviews stay out of my way and I'll stay out of yours. Now that we understand each other, maybe we'll be able to tolerate each other."

He released her hand and opened the door, shoving it wide. She jerked free of his pressing weight against her side and stepped out onto the hot pavement. She slammed the door behind her, then stood in impotent rage as his tires squealed away in a shower of gravel, leaving her in a cloud of white, powdery dust.

Ten minutes later she was met at the front door of the house by a woman who could only be Gracie. Apparently Lyon had had enough decency to alert both the housekeeper and the guard at the gate that she would be arriving within minutes.

"You look like you need to freshen up before lunch," Gracie said commiseratingly. "It's so hot out, isn't it? Come on upstairs and I'll show you to your room. I've never seen the general so excited. He told me to roll out the red carpet. You've been given the largest bedroom upstairs, except for Lyon's, of course."

Gracie Halstead, as she introduced herself, was ample of bosom and thick in the waist. Her grey hair and happy, round face gave her a maternal aspect, as did her coddling mannerisms. "Here we are," she said, opening the

43

door to an airy room filled with antique furniture and bright sunlight.

The room faced the south side of the house. Rolling hills reached out to the horizon. Whiteface Hereford cattle grazed in the lush pastures. Through the nearest pasture a river wound its way across the Ratliff property. Graceful cypress trees with their feathery foliage and twisted, rope-like trunks lined the banks of the river.

"That's the Guadalupe you're looking at."

"It's beautiful here," Andy said, meaning to include everything, the view, the room, the house.

"Yep. I've lived here since General Ratliff built this house soon after the war. I never tire of looking at the view. Did you see the pool? The general says you're to use any and all of the facilities while you're here."

"Thank you. I will."

"Lyon brought up your bags." She nodded toward the luggage that Andy imagined had been thumped unceremoniously onto the hardwood floor.

"Yes. Kind of him." Her sarcasm escaped Gracie.

"I'll get back downstairs now and hustle up some lunch. The bathroom's through there." She indicated a door. "I outfitted it, but if I missed something, you come to the top of the stairs and holler real loud."

Andy laughed. "Okay."

Gracie smiled, crossing her arms over her stomach, tilting her head to one side, and appraising Andy from the top of her head to her feet. Obviously she liked what she saw. "I think the general was right. I think it's going to be . . . interesting having you here." Before Andy could puzzle out that enigmatic statement, Gracie went on to say, "Lunch is at noon."

Then she was gone and Andy was alone. She stripped out of the wrinkled suit that until this morning had been fresh from the dry cleaners. She shook it free of what dust she could, muttering aspersions on the character of Lyon Ratliff.

After a quick, refreshing shower in the beautiful bathroom, which was decorated in shades of yellow and butterscotch, she dressed in a casual skirt and polo shirt.

She took her hairbrush to the window and took down her hair. As she gazed at the scenery from her vantage point on the second floor Lyon came around the side of the garage. He joined Mr. Houghton, who was kneeling in the flower beds, still planting the new shrubbery.

The hairbrush was held motionless above her head as Lyon pulled his shirttail from the waistband of his jeans and proceeded to unbutton his shirt. He peeled the shirt away from his chest and shoulders, and then hung it on the lowest branch of a pecan tree. Absorbed as he was in his conversation with Mr. Houghton, his motions were natural and unaffected, yet executed as though they were steps in a seductive ballet.

Andy's hand covered her breast lest her heart burst through. Her speculations on what lay beneath Lyon's shirt hadn't prepared her for seeing it in the flesh. His shoulders were wide and rippled with lean muscles as he picked up the handles of a wheelbarrow and pushed it forward several yards. His chest was matted with dark, crisp hair that fanned out over the upper part of his torso and tapered to a sleek arrow that disappeared into his jeans. Andy's stomach did an erratic dance when he idly scratched at a rib with his long slender fingers.

He laughed at something Mr. Houghton said and she was struck by how white his teeth looked against his dark face. The corners of his eyes crinkled into a humorous expression she'd never seen before. She had only seen him angry and insulting, hateful and vehement.

No. There was one other way she had seen him. Suggestive and insolent.

Checking her watch, she stepped away from the window and put the forgotten hairbrush aside. Apparently Lyon wasn't coming in to lunch.

He didn't, but Andy enjoyed the green salad Gracie had made for her. It was heaped with grated cheese and cold sliced turkey.

"You look like you eat a lot of salads," the housekeeper observed. "And that's all right at lunch, but I'm going to see to it personally that you're fattened up while you're here."

"Please don't go to any trouble for me. You'll have your hands full when my crew arrives. We'll create chaos in your spotless, serene house. I can only promise you that we'll try to be as unobtrusive and neat as possible."

"There's never been a mess in this house I couldn't clean up. You do whatever you have to do."

"With your permission, General Ratliff, I'll spend this afternoon prowling around, looking for the best locations to shoot the interviews."

He was sitting at the head of the table, picking at his plate of bland food. "Certainly. You have the run of the house."

"Where are you most comfortable?"

"I spend most of my time in the sun room where you found me this morning," he said, giving her a wink. "Or in my bedroom. Sometimes I sit in the living room."

"I want you to be in a natural environment so you'll be relaxed when the cameras roll. I'll need to check out those rooms for electrical outlets, and such. Tonight I'll call Nashville to tell the crew what equipment to bring. They'll probably be arriving the day after tomorrow."

She spent several hours that afternoon examining the rooms the general had mentioned, looking not only for the most advantageous settings technically, but aesthetically as well. One thing her audience had come to expect from an Andy Malone interview was that it was scrupulously researched and planned.

Gracie provided her with a box of clippings and memorabilia that chronicled the general's life and career in the Army. She went through the contents carefully, noticing that the newspaper articles were dated to within a few years after the war. At that time he had taken an early retirement and become the recluse he had remained for over thirty years. Her reporter's mind homed in on that fact, but beyond the sudden cessation of publicity, she could see no significance to it. She filled two sheets of a legal pad with possible questions.

Guessing correctly that dinner wouldn't be a formal affair, she only changed her blouse. The one she selected was an ecru georgette with a short flutter sleeve. The narrow lapels dipped deeply before buttoning together just above her decolletage. She left her hair to fall free around her shoulders.

Lyon, looking damply clean from a recent shower, was securing his father's wheelchair at the end of the table when she entered the dining room. He looked up and their eyes met and held for an inordinate length of time before she mumbled a "Good evening."

He was, of course, fully clothed, but she could still see him as he had looked bare-chested. Her pulse sped up perceptibly when he graciously held her chair for her, and the scent that she realized was uniquely his washed over her.

Through the fog of sensations that assailed her it occurred to her that she should be furious with him. The last time they had met face to face he had been blatantly rude and insulting. He had left her to choke on his dust as he deserted her on the highway. To her irritation, instead of rekindling her anger, the sight of him had only produced that shaky, hollow feeling deep inside that had plagued her since she first saw him.

The general, oblivious to or ignoring the tension between his son and their guest, bowed his head to say grace. Andy and Lyon followed suit. A few seconds into the prayer Andy yielded to the temptation to look at Lyon, who was seated directly across from her. Long, dark lashes unveiled her eyes slowly, then sprang wide when her eyes clashed with steady gray ones that were staring at her without a modicum of timidity or shame. To avoid their hypnotic power, she quickly squeezed her eyes shut and bowed her head again.

"Andy began choosing sites for the interviews today," the general said after Gracie had served Lyon and Andy. Another plate of food that looked entirely unpalatable had been set before the general. The housekeeper was making good her promise to fatten Andy up. The food was sumptuous and plentiful.

"Oh?" One of Lyon's black brows cocked with interest.

"Yes," she said. "Your father was gracious enough to give me carte blanche to use all the rooms of the house." She had intended that as a rebuke for his own inhospitality, but saw that she had failed. The corner of his mouth twitched with amusement. "However, I think we'll confine the shooting to rooms that your father frequents ordinarily." She looked toward General Ratliff. "Is it possible for you to go outside? I'd like to do some exterior shooting for B roll."

"B roll?" Lyon asked.

"B roll is an additional tape with an alternate scene. It can get rather boring to watch two people sitting in two chairs for thirty minutes. But if we have some B roll, we can electronically edit it into the interview segment."

Lyon nodded with comprehension.

"Lyon was thoughtful enough to pave a path to the river to accommodate the wheelchair when I became too infirm to walk down there. Would the bank of the river be a good setting?" the general asked.

"Yes! Perfect."

"Good. Lyon will take you down there after dinner, and you can check it out."

Chapter Three

❧

I 'm sure Lyon has other things to do," Andy mumbled into her plate, not daring to look at the man across the table from her.

"Not a thing," he said.

Her fork clattered onto the china. She strove to keep her voice calm. "It would be much more practical to see things in the daylight," she said to the general, still not acknowledging that Lyon had consented to his father's suggestion.

"No doubt. But you've been cooped up in the house all day and haven't even looked around the grounds. The walk will do you good. Now finish your apple pie so you can get started."

She looked at Lyon, hoping that he would support her, but he looked like the proverbial cat who had swallowed the canary. Couldn't he have thought up an excuse why he couldn't walk with her? She speared one of the fat apple slices in Gracie's pie as she glowered at him. Of course he could have. He was only looking forward to another opportunity to ridicule her. This time he would be disappointed. She wasn't going to rise to the bait, no matter how provoking he became.

"Lyon, on your way out would you please ask Gracie to bring me some warm milk in my room?" the general asked. "I'm very tired tonight."

Andy instantly forgot her problems with Lyon and turned her concerned attention to the man who had brought her to this house in the first place.

"Are you not feeling well, Dad?" Lyon asked. "Should I call Dr. Baker?"

"No, no. I'm not feeling anything but eighty-some-odd years old. I'm going to bed now and get a good night's sleep. I want to look my best when Andy interviews me." He winked at her again. Impulsively she got up and, leaning over his wheelchair, kissed him on the cheek.

"Goodnight, General Ratliff."

"Forget the warm milk, Lyon, I think I can go right to sleep now." He waved good night and then steered his chair out of the room.

"Can he . . . do . . . for himself? See to his needs?" she asked softly.

Lyon's sigh was sad and resigned. "Yes." He rubbed the back of his neck with a weary hand. "He insists that he still dress and undress himself, though I know it exhausts him. He's proud. He wouldn't even agree to a male nurse." His look was bleak as he stared at the empty doorway through which his father had just passed, and Andy knew that the son loved the father and vice versa. After a moment he shook his head slightly and looked down at her. "Are you finished with your pie?"

She pinched off one last morsel of the fluted crust and popped it into her mouth. "Delicious," she exclaimed, daintily flicking her tongue across the tips of her fingers to rid them of crumbs. When all had been thoroughly cleaned, she looked up at him smilingly.

The breath caught in her throat and her smile dissolved into the partially opened lips of a woman about to be kissed. Lyon stared at her mouth with single-minded concentration, and it was impossible not to respond to his heated gaze. She felt herself gravitating toward him. His magnetism was as potent as the moon's pull on the tide, and it was as futile to resist.

"I think you missed some," he said hoarsely. Lifting her hand to his mouth, he drew her fingers toward his lips.

My God, her mind screamed. *If he does it, I'll die*. Yet at that moment she couldn't think of anything more electrifying than having his tongue bathe each of her fingertips with gentle, wet strokes.

His eyes locked onto hers and refused to let go. But instead of licking her fingertips, he blew on them gently until the tiny flakes of pastry gave up their tenuous hold.

Her heart knocked painfully against her ribs. What little breath had been momentarily trapped in her throat was expelled on a shuddering sigh. Then it was impossible to draw any more in, and her lungs constricted against the emptiness. She only hoped she had been able to stifle the soft moan that had pressed against her vocal cords before it could be uttered.

"Lyon, Andy, are you finished?" He dropped her hand and took a step backward as Gracie pushed her way through the swinging door that connected the dining room to the kitchen. "Would you like your coffee on the patio?"

"We're going to walk down to the river," he answered with more calm than Andy could have mustered at that moment. "Why don't you have it waiting for us when we get back? I don't know how long we'll be, so go on to bed if you want."

"I'll wash up these dishes and check on General Ratliff," Gracie said. "Your coffee will be waiting for you on the patio, and if I don't see you later, good night."

"Good night, Gracie," Lyon said.

"Good night and thank you for the delicious dinner," Andy said, hoping the housekeeper wouldn't notice her high color.

"You're welcome. Now you two scoot out of my way. Get on with your walk."

Lyon led the way through Gracie's domain, the kitchen. It was enormous, and stainless-steel, commercial-sized appliances lined the walls.

"Does she cook for all your hands in here?" Andy knew that the Ratliff ranch was like a small city. Dozens of cowboys and their families lived within its boundaries.

"For years she cooked for the single men who live in the bunkhouse. He indicated a dormitory-looking building to the left as they went through the patio door. "But when Dad got so ill, I hired a cook for that kitchen. Gracie's main responsibility now is to look after Dad when I'm not around."

"You said this morning that she'd been here longer than you."

"Yes, she came to this house with Mom and Dad when it was built. Mom died when I was ten. Gracie's seen to me ever since."

"What was your mother like?" They were walking down the path toward the river, having skirted the pool and a few of the many outbuildings that made up the compound. Andy noted that the shrubbery Mr. Houghton had planted looked very well. An earthy, mossy smell from the freshly turned and dampened soil permeated the night air.

It was a beautiful night. The crescent moon looked like a prop for a stage play, perfectly suspended over the distant hills. A southern breeze lifted the hair away from Andy's face as she walked with Lyon under the canopy of pecan and live oak branches.

"It's sad, but I remember incidents rather than the person. My impressions of Mom are gentleness, kindness, warmth. But maybe all children think of their mothers that way." He smiled, and his teeth shone even in the deepening shadows. "I remember that she always smelled a particular way. I'm not sure I've ever smelled that perfume before or since, but I'd know her by that fragrance even now. Her name was Rosemary."

"Yes, I read that today in some of the clippings. Your father was said to have been very diligent during the war about writing home to her. They must have been very close."

"They were. Rarely so." The bitterness in his voice couldn't be masked, and he quickly changed the subject. "What about your parents?"

"Mother lives in Indianapolis. Father died several years ago."

"What did he do?"

"He was a journalist. He was quite popular in the area. His column was syndicated in several newspapers."

"So your interest in journalism began at an early age."

Was that his first attempt to get a rise out of her? "Yes, I guess so," she answered smoothly.

The gentle roar of the river caught her attention, and she realized that they had arrived at the grassy banks that sloped downward. She peered into the swirling clear waters that churned over limestone boulders in the riverbed. "Oh, Lyon, it's lovely," she cried excitedly.

"You like it?"

"It's wonderful! The water looks so clear."

"In the daytime you can see that it is. It washes over and filters through miles of limestone. This is some of the purest water in the state."

"And the trees. They're beautiful," she said, tilting her head back to look through the delicate branches of the cypress at a starry sky. "You love it, don't you? This land."

"Yes. I suppose some would have thought that I'd go in for a military career like my father. But he had retired from the Army before I was old enough to realize he was ever anything but a rancher. We've lived here all my life. I did my stint in Nam, but went into the Army hoping no one would connect me with my famous father. Soldiering wasn't for me."

"You ranch."

"I ranch. I also own some commercial real estate. But this is what I love," he said, sweeping his arms wide to encompass the landscape.

"It's a shame there's only the two of you to share it." She made the comment without thinking and regretted it the moment she said it. It was too much to ask that he would overlook it.

"If you wanted to ask why I've never married, why didn't you just come right out with it, Ms. Malone? I'd never expect you to mince words."

"I didn't—"

"For your information," he said tightly, "I was married. The debacle lasted four miserable years. When she got bored with the ranch, the house, my father, and me, she left, bag and baggage. I never saw her again. She got a divorce through Uncle Sam's postal service and Alexander Graham Bell's marvelous invention."

"And now you take out your hatred for her on the rest of the female population." She had been leaning against the trunk of the cypress. Now she pushed herself angrily erect.

"No. You have to have some feelings for someone before you can hate him. Whatever feelings I had for her died the moment she left. Let's just say that I distrust the female of the species."

"Then you'll go down as a confirmed old bachelor?"

"Most definitely."

"Surely the ladies in Kerrville aren't going to stand for that," she said provocatively, remembering the motel clerk's interest when Lyon had picked her up. "Don't they hound you to find yourself a suitable mate?"

"Yes. Every mother with a deb has thrown her daughter at me. I've been hopefully introduced to every divorcee in town. It was even conveniently arranged that I share a table at a dinner party with a young widow whose husband had been dead less than a month."

"So you spurn all women."

He came up from his slouching position against a boulder and took a few steps forward until only a hairs-breadth separated them. "No, I don't *spurn* women. I just said that I don't *marry* them. I'm plagued—or maybe blessed is a better word—with the same carnal drives as any man over the age of fifteen."

His words had now taken on a different tone: Gone were the clipped, laconic phrases of a man who had endured the whims of a frivolous woman. In their place were the low-timbred vibrations of a man aroused.

Andy wet her dry, trembling lips and pivoted away from him to look down into the river. "I . . . I think this will be a good location to shoot the outdoor scenes. Of course, the noise of the water has to be dealt with, but—" Her chattering broke off abruptly when she felt his hands on her shoulders. Large hands. Hard. Strong. Tender. Hot. He turned her around.

"You've been dying of curiosity, haven't you?" His breath was a warm vapor coasting over her face.

"Curiosity?" she squeaked and hated herself for the immature sound. "About what?"

"About me."

"What about you?"

"About what it's like to be touched, kissed, by a red-neck cowboy. That's what you thought of me the first time you saw me, didn't you?"

"No," she said, untruthfully. Men like him were rare in the circles she ran in. Men like him were rare, period. He was a novelty, but she hadn't realized she had let him know she thought of him as such.

He went on in a voice that could have melted butter, which was exactly what she felt like. "You didn't take your returned, unopened letters as a no, so you thought you'd come down here and sweet-talk a dumb hick into letting you interview his father. You thought I'd dissolve like mush when I got a look at your golden eyes and your creamy skin and your silky hair and your sexy body, didn't you?"

"No!" she cried softly, earnestly. He wasn't being fair. She recognized the insincerity of his embrace, yet she yearned for a closer one. Even as he mocked her, she craved his touch.

"And the more I insulted you, the more curious you became, until I was getting to you real bad. Do you think I didn't know you were watching me today? Did you see anything you *didn't* like?"

Thankfully, mercifully, her temper flared and she was given a chance to save herself. "You conceited—"

"Brace yourself, Ms. Malone. I'm about to satisfy your curiosity. Among other things."

Using his size to overpower her, he walked them backward until once again her back was against the cypress tree's trunk. Deftly, boldly, he unbuttoned the first button of her blouse. Then the second.

She stared directly into his eyes, her chin raised and pointed with disdain. She only hoped he couldn't feel her treacherous heartbeat. "I'm not going to dignify this by fighting or struggling."

"Fight or struggle if you like. You won't stop me. And I don't give a damn if it's dignified or not."

Then his mouth bore down on hers, and the battle was lost before it was ever joined. His lips were firm, but curiously soft as they slanted over hers. He moved them in such a way that hers opened involuntarily before she was aware of it.

For prolonged moments he hesitated, breathing into her mouth, making her ache with anticipation—never dread. Then his tongue glided over her bottom lip, the top one, slipped between them, coaxing her mouth to accept its skillful violation ... He swept the interior triumphantly. But suddenly he lifted his head.

His eyes impaled her. His uneven breathing was an echo of hers. Two hearts beat together. He scanned her face. What was he searching for? She looked up at him with a silent plea. Then, as though directed by a master choreographer, his arms closed about her at the same time she locked her hands behind his neck.

When his mouth descended again, hers was open and waiting to receive it. This kiss was no longer motivated by a challenge, but by a mutual hunger that threatened to destroy them should they not appease it. His tongue sampled each nuance of her mouth with a fervent desperation, as though she were some elusive dream that might vanish before he'd had his fill.

He tore his mouth free at last, and she collapsed against him. His lips wandered at random over her face, dropping brief kisses wherever they alit. Her fingers knotted in his hair, holding his head against her as he nuzzled her neck.

"Lyon," she breathed when his hands came around her rib cage, the heels of them brushing the sides of her breasts. Moving slowly, his hands parted the unbuttoned blouse and covered her breasts with possessive warmth.

He squeezed her gently. Lifting her up, he tested the fullness and found it gratifying. The satin camisole was worn for modesty's sake beneath the sheer blouse. But it provided no shelter from his seductive caresses, and her nipples responded firmly and proudly to the stroking of his thumbs.

His mouth was at her ear, lazily nipping the lobe with his teeth. "What do you know? I've found something about you that isn't phony."

If he had slapped her, she couldn't be more stunned. She grabbed his wrists and pulled his hands away from her, shoving him backward with surprising strength. "Is that all this was to you? An experiment?!" she shouted.

"Wasn't that all it was to you?" he asked with deliberate, mocking indifference.

"God, you're disgusting." She stumbled past him, frantically adjusting her clothing in the night that had suddenly gone dark and cold. She was yanked around by his painful grip on her upper arm. Every inch of his tall body radiated fury.

"Me? I didn't invade anyone's home, looking for secrets and skeletons in the closet."

"I—"

"My father may have been hoodwinked by you, but not me, sister. I know your type—"

"Stop saying that," she screamed. "I'm not a *type*. Can't you get that through that thick head of yours? I came here to do an interview with your father. I know he's ill. I'm sensitive to that, but that's all the more reason I want to remind the American people about him, because he may not be around forever. Why you indicted, convicted, and were ready to hang me before you even met me, I don't know. But I'm here. And I'll do my job in spite of you. With or without your cooperation." She could feel scalding tears clogging her throat and flooding her eyes and was only glad that the darkness obscured them from him. "Finally, don't touch me again." She flung off his hand that was like a manacle around her arm.

"You can bet on it," he said bitingly. "One kiss in the dark doesn't make you a woman, Ms. Malone. You're ambitious, shrewd, headstrong. You're just an imitation of a man living in a female body, without any of the softness or gentleness or kindness that should characterize your sex."

His words stung. For years she had felt just like the shell he'd described. She protested vehemently. "I'm not. I'm *not*."

"You couldn't prove it by me."

"I don't want to." But she did, and that humiliating fact filled her mouth like brassy-tasting medicine as she stalked back toward the house.

"Did I wake you?" she said into the telephone receiver. The house had been quiet when she arrived back, though Gracie had left the promised coffee on the patio table. It went untouched. Glad that she didn't have to face anyone, she had made her way upstairs without turning on any lights. She had bathed in the deep, claw-footed bathtub, hoping to wash away the memory of the hour she had spent with Lyon. It would take more than a bath to do that. Still feeling shame and anger, she had pulled on a robe and padded into the hallway to place her call to Les.

"Hell, no. I wish you had. I'm only about halfway to getting stinking drunk. And halfway doesn't count."

"What the matter? No date tonight?"

"My best girl's out of town," he grumbled. She laughed, knowing he wasn't serious. "You just want to be mothered."

"I could get to feeling downright oedipal about you, Andy Malone." He sighed, and she could imagine him raking his hand through his bright hair. "I'll bet you're down there whooping it up with all the cowboys."

She ignored his jibe. He had no idea how true it might have been. Lyon had kissed her with such tenderness, such passion. How could he have . . .? She gulped down a sob. "Then you're not interested in knowing that I'm now in residence at the Ratliffs' ranch house?"

"You're wh—" There was a loud crash at the other end of the line, some blasphemous language, then Les's voice, much sharper and clearer now. She had sobered him up. "I dropped the phone. You're *what*? Living there? With the old man? Have you met him yet? What about the son?"

"One at a time, Les. Yes, at the general's invitation I'm staying here. And so will the crew be. They've been offered beds in the bunkhouse."

"Godamighty. I knew you could pull it off, sweet thing."

"General Ratliff is a perfect gentleman. He's agreed to the interviews, though we have to be careful about tiring him. He's extremely frail, Les."

"But he's said yes to the interviews?"

"Yes."

"And the son?"

Had Les not been so excited by her news, he might have noticed the significant pause. "He's less enthusiastic, but I don't think he'll interfere with us."

"Great, fabulous, terrific. If I were there right now, I'd give you a kiss that'd ring your bells and make your toes curl."

She trembled. She'd already had one kiss that had done that tonight. It had been the first kiss in her life that had affected her that intensely. She had been totally involved in Lyon, his mouth, his taste, his smell, his touch, the alignment of his body against hers. She and Robert had been an affectionate couple, at first, but . . .

"Andy baby, are you still there?"

"Y—yes."

"Well, tell me all about it, doll."

"The general's very friendly, grandfatherly, or great grandfatherly. He said I could ask him about anything except specific battles. His—"

"Whoa, whoa, go back. What was that about specific et cetera?"

"He said he wouldn't answer questions pertaining to specific battles, only to the war as a whole."

"Curiouser and curiouser."

"Why?"

"Have you ever heard of a military man, especially a general, who *didn't* want to tell war stories? Do you think the old codger has something to hide?"

Not only his suspicion, but his unflattering term for Michael Ratliff irritated her. "No," she said flatly. "I don't think so. I read through piles of newspapers clippings today, dated from early in his career to the day he retired. There was never even the hint of a scandal of any kind."

"Well, it bears thinking about."

She wouldn't think about it at all. If there were something unsavory in General Ratliff's past, she didn't want to know about it. "I scouted through the house today, which is lovely and will give us some great background shots. We'll confine the interviews to the rooms the general feels most comfortable in. And I want to do some outside shooting. Tell Gil to bring along some kind of mike sock that will filter out the roar of water."

"Water? What in the hell, Andy?"

"A river."

"A river. Okay what else? I'm making a list."

She went on to tell him about the set up and what the crew would need to bring as far as cables and lights and battery packs and microphones were concerned.

"I guess that's everything," she said after she'd gone over everything listed on her note pad.

"Not quite," Les said shortly.

"What else?"

"You could tell me why you sound like a sorority girl who's just discovered she's out of birth control pills the day before the big weekend."

"Les," she groaned. She'd never get used to his ribaldry. "Nothing's wrong. It's awfully hot—"

"So was Florida when you interviewed those Cuban refugees. You were exhilarated by that interview. What's going on down there?"

The last thing she needed was Les's nose, which was a mile long when it came to sniffing out discrepancies of any kind, prying into her ambiguous feelings for Lyon. Les could always be diverted with flattery. "Did you ever stop to think that I'm homesick, that I miss you?"

"Uh-huh, like a dog misses fleas."

"No."

"Back to that later. I'm still hung up on this general not wanting to talk about those battles."

"Les, please. It's nothing. He probably doesn't want to relive the whole war in detail, that's all."

"What about the son? Think he'd talk?"

"No," she said sharply.

"Wow! Did I strike a nerve? What's this son like anyway?"

"He's . . . he's like nothing. I mean he's an intelligent businessman, a rancher, who has no interest in military matters. He told me that himself."

"But he has an interest in his old man. And if the old man has something to hide, so does the son. Think you can wheedle it out of him?"

"No, Les. I wouldn't try even if there *were* something, which I'm sure there's *not*."

"Come on, Andy baby, don't go all naïve and Pollyanna on me. You know as well as I do that *everyone* has something to hide. Go to work on the son. God, if you practiced one tenth of your technique on me, I'd babble like a brook."

"I don't have a technique."

"You damn well do, you're just too nice to know it." He let that sink in, then continued. "Warm up to the son, Andy. You can do it for me. Okay?" She said nothing. "You're probably right about no secrets, but it never hurts to make friends, does it? Say you'll try your tricks on the son . . . Lyon, is it? Okay?"

"Okay, okay, I'll see what I can do." She had every intention of staying as far away from Lyon Ratliff as possible, but she was only telling Les what he wanted to hear to keep the peace. "I've got to go now."

"Darlin', you saved me from a hellish hangover tomorrow. How can I ever thank you?"

"You'll think of something," she said dryly.

"I already have, but you'd never go for it. I love ya. You know that, don't you?"

Les must truly be depressed tonight and craving sympathy. "Yes, I know you love me, Les, and I love you, too."

"Then I'll say good night."

"Good night."

"Sweet dreams."

"Sweet dreams to you, too."

She hung up, feeling that she'd been put through a wringer. First by Lyon and now by Les. But Lyon had hurt her more. She was accustomed to Les's swift changes of mood, his whining, his lechery, his exuberance, which tired anyone out who didn't share it.

Pausing only long enough to switch off the light as she entered her room, she went directly to her bed. She fell onto the scented sheets and pulled the light covers over her. Reviewing the day, she couldn't believe all that had happened. Had she behaved irresponsibly and impulsively to pull that trick of getting in to see the general? Had she gone about it another way, had she approached Lyon like a professional, would he feel differently toward her? Probably not. She had tried that tack yesterday. He had drawn his conclusions about her long before then.

It was obvious that he was projecting his wife's faults onto all women. She had been flighty and selfish. She had left him for greener pastures, and he hadn't gone after her. That wasn't surprising. A man like Lyon wouldn't go chasing after a woman who had left him. His wife hadn't been happy with hearth and home, so he assumed every woman who pursued a career was as heartless and fickle as she had been.

"That isn't necessarily so, Mr. Ratliff," she said to the dark shadows in the room.

Some choices are made for people by others. Andrea Malone had never considered a career outside journalism because her father had wanted it for her so badly. Having no brothers, she had been the anointed one to carry on his name in the field. She had married Robert, and when her father died, she was almost relieved that now she could settle down and devote her time and energies to a home and family.

Robert had been surprised and amused when she outlined her plans to him. "You can't mean that you're going to quit work and become a homebody." His face had registered his astonishment. It was apparent the idea had never occurred to him.

She had smiled tensely. "Don't you want to have children?"

"Well, yeah, sure, Andy. But only after we're too old to do everything else. I like having my wife on the tube. We get great seats in restaurants, passes to the movies, and I get to claim that I sleep with the famous Andy Malone."

Often Andy felt that Robert considered her a trophy— a trophy that was only treasured each night in the bedroom. Because she felt that way, she often couldn't respond to him. The trophy began to tarnish. Robert had grabbed at the job for the network and was away from home almost constantly, inventing stories to cover when he wasn't assigned one. Then he had been killed.

Andy knew that if she had not made him unhappy, he might not have gone to Guatemala. Lyon was right. She was on a guilt trip. She felt she owed it to Robert to prove him right, to live up to his expectations. She wasn't made to be a wife and mother, but a career woman. For three years she had kept herself insulated by her work. All her attention had been concentrated on furthering her career. She had almost become convinced that she didn't want a man and his love, that she didn't need it, that she could live without it.

But her eyes had locked with Lyon Ratliff's over Gabe Sander's Formica counter top, and she knew then that she *did* want a man. He had touched her and created a need.

And now, after his kiss, her body was transmitting a hundred sensual messages to her brain that she may very well die if she didn't have him.

"Good morning, Andy. You slept well, I hope."

"Yes," she lied. "Thank you, General. I didn't know if breakfast was a ritual or not. I'm afraid I was rather lazy this morning."

"I'm allowed to be lazy every morning, and I hate it. I'd much rather be up with the dawn the way Lyon is. What would you like?" he asked her as Gracie came into the dining room carrying the general's breakfast tray, which looked as unappetizing as all his meals.

Gracie brought in the coffee, juice, and one piece of wheat toast, as requested, *tsk*ing and shaking her head in disapproval of such a meager breakfast.

"What are your plans today, Andy?" Michael Ratliff asked her just as she was finishing her coffee.

"I need to go over my notes again, to rephrase them into the questions I'll ask during each segment. That way I won't repeat myself, though I'm sure your answers will generate questions I haven't even thought of. By the way, the crew is flying into San Antonio tonight and will be here first thing tomorrow morning."

"I think you're working too hard. Lyon asked for you to meet him outside when you're finished with breakfast." The old man's eyes were sparkling. "I think he'd like to take you for a ride."

Chapter Four

Aride?"

"Around the ranch. You'd like to see it, wouldn't you?" Andy couldn't disappoint the general, who was obviously proud of his ranch and wanted her to see it. "Yes, I do, but I'm here to work, not to be entertained. I don't want to take up Lyon's time. Surely he has better things to do."

"He might have *other* things to do. I doubt if he'd consider any of them *better*," Michael Ratliff said, smiling.

She couldn't imagine that Lyon wanted to see her any more than she wanted to see him after what had happened last night. "Are you sure he asked to see me?"

"That was the last thing he said before he left. He asked that you meet him near the garage. Now if you'll excuse me, Andy, I spend my mornings reading. I can only read for a while before my eyes give out. We'll talk after lunch if you like."

"Yes, and please rest. The next few days will be arduous."

"I'll have a long time to rest, Andy," he said dryly. "I'm looking forward to the interviews." He wheeled out of the room.

She finished her coffee in solitude, trying to marshal enough mental and physical fortitude to face Lyon. What did one wear to tour a ranch? To save herself from derision, she wasn't going to wear her jeans and western boots again. She decided that the casual slacks and knit top she was wearing were as appropriate as anything.

Let him wait, she thought perversely as she went upstairs to check her hair and makeup. Picking up an atomizer of her favorite perfume, she studied it a moment, then sprayed herself liberally. If he read anything into it, he would be wrong. She always wore fragrance, even in the daytime.

The patio and pool area were deserted when she stepped through the glass door. The morning smelled fresh and felt cool. Clouds were shading the sun and a gentle southern breeze was stirring the leaves of the trees. Standing very still and listening, she could hear the gurgling of the river.

"Good morning."

She jumped and spun around. She had been so intent on the beauty of her surroundings that she hadn't heard him come up behind her. "Good morning." He was

74

wearing fragrance, too. That same brisk, clean scent she was coming to associate with him.

"Ready?"

"Yes." He turned his back on her and walked stiffly toward a parked Jeep she hadn't noticed until now. It was without doors. There was no top over it, only a roll bar, and the seats looked as though the Jeep had been driven over many a dusty trail. Lyon slumped into the driver's seat, and she climbed into the passenger side. She barely had time to get a good handhold before he accelerated and the Jeep lurched forward. He had a lot to learn about the subtleties of good driving.

"Sleep okay?"

"Yes," she lied, for the second time that morning. She didn't want to see the sinewy strength of his arm as he shoved the gearshift into higher gear. His legs worked the pedals of the vehicle with a flexing of thigh muscles that was awesome. She diverted her eyes from his lap, the sight of which made a tumbling team of her vital organs.

His hands gripped the steering wheel hard. There was an aspect of controlled violence about him this morning. Every thread of his clothing seemed strained to contain the tension just under his skin.

She studied his face beneath the brim of his straw cowboy hat. The lines of his jaw were as hard as iron. When he blinked, it was more than nature's way of moistening his eyes. It was reflex of anger, as though he were trying to clear his vision that had been clouded with rage.

He seemed disinclined to talk as he concentrated on keeping the bouncing Jeep on the uneven trail. Andy turned away from him and studied the landscape. She'd be damned if she'd force her company on him. After the disgraceful thing he had done the evening before, he should be thankful she'd speak to him at all. If he held her in such contempt, why had he suggested this outing?

Damn her! Lyon thought. All ten fingers extended as the palms of his hands rested on the wheel. He stretched them out as far as they would go, then curled them around the steering wheel in so tight a grip, they ached.

If she had to be who she was, why did she have to look like she did? If she wanted to move in a man's world, why didn't she dress the part? Why did she wear clothes like that shirt-thing she had on now that molded to each soft curve of her breast? And pants that hugged her bottom? And why were her feet bare in sandals so skimpy that he marveled over how she kept them on her feet. Her toenails were polished with a delicate shade of coral. Like the color only found inside a seashell . . .

Hell! he cursed. *Would you listen to yourself, Ratliff? Seashells! God.*

So she's a great-looking broad. So? Do you have to act as imbecilic as an adolescent? You've been with good-looking women before, some even more beautiful than this one. But there's something about . . .

Her eyes? Unusual color, yes, but . . . No, it's the way she looks at you when you're talking to her. It's as if what you're saying is of vital importance to her. She's interested. She wants to know. Your opinion matters to her.

Easy, Ratliff. Don't be too taken in by that. Isn't that what she's supposed to make you feel? Isn't that her job? The secret of being a good interviewer is the ability to listen.

Okay, so her eyes are pretty and she uses them to full advantage. You still know that she lies with that luscious mouth. If not with words, then certainly with kisses. Face it, buddy, a kiss hasn't meant that much to you in a long time. Some women fake passion, hoping to get to your checkbook. Most respond out of conditioned reflex because they know it'll please you if they do. But Andy . . . hell, yes, go ahead and think her name. *Andy. Andy.* Her passion hadn't been faked. She needed that kiss as badly as you did. She wanted it.

She'd known how to give and how to take. You felt desire rocketing through you until you were ready to explode. It scared you, and you swore that you wouldn't have anything more to do with her. And then the first thing you do this morning is arrange to see her alone.

She's poison, dammit. So why are you watching her out of the corner of your eye, Ratliff? Why are you looking at her hand that's gripping the edge of her seat with every bump. Are you hoping that since it's so close to your thigh that she'll . . .

Lyon jerked his thoughts back from where they were wandering and braked the Jeep suddenly. Inertia propelled them forward until they fell back against the seats.

Andy looked over the bluff. The scenery was beautiful. They had climbed into the hills and were now gazing down at the valley. The house looked like a toy far beneath them, nestled in the grove beside the river.

She wished he'd say something. Was he waiting for her to speak? She turned her head slightly to look at him. He was staring over the hood of the Jeep. "It's beautiful up here," she said tentatively.

He pushed the cowboy hat back far on his head and without moving his body, swiveled his head around to stab her with his eyes. "Who is Les?"

It wasn't so much the question itself as the way he asked it that made her feel like she'd been punched in the stomach. She suffered all the symptoms of having sustained a stunning blow and having the breath knocked out of her. She sucked air greedily. "He's my boss."

"How convenient."

"What do you mean?"

"I mean, do you carry on in the office or do you wait until work is done for the day? Does he know you were out in the woods last night letting another man kiss and fondle you, or would he care? Maybe it's one of those 'open' relationships."

Her cheeks flamed crimson, first at his allusion to last night and then with anger. "There *is* no relationship other than friendship."

"Don't lie to me, dammit. I heard you. 'I know you love me, and I love you, too.' "

"You eavesdropped!?"

"I overheard. You were out in the hallway, you know, and you weren't speaking in whispers. I was on my way upstairs. Of course I heard you."

My God. How much had he heard? If he'd heard her promising Les she'd work on the son for information— No, he wasn't quizzing her about that. He wanted to know about her and Les. But why? If it weren't so ridiculous, she'd think he was jealous. Actually it must only be male pride. She was sure few women had fled Lyon's arms to go call another man and tell him she loved him. "A gentleman would have made his presence known."

He laughed harshly. "I quit being a gentleman a long time ago. Well, I'm waiting. Tell me about this Les."

Why didn't she tell him it was none of his business and order him to take her back to the house? Because for some unnamed reason, it was important that he did not misconstrue her relationship with Les. She'd examine the why of that later, when he wasn't looking at her with such sanctimonious outrage.

Composure would be her counterattack. She wouldn't countenance his anger, merely show that she was tolerating it, much as a parent tolerates the temper tantrum of a willful child. "Les Trapper is the producer of my show. We've worked together for years, before, during, and after I was married. He's a friend. As for my telling him I love him, I do. As a friend. He tells every woman he meets from high-school girls to the elderly lady who cleans our offices that he loves her. It means nothing. At no point have Les and I been lovers."

"Do you expect me to believe that?"

Her composure snapped. "I don't give a damn whether you do or not. You branded a scarlet letter on my breast the moment I introduced myself to you." She wished she hadn't referred to her breast. His eyes dropped significantly to that region of her torso. Undaunted, she went on. "Just because I'm not a homemaker, doesn't mean that I have no morals, Mr. Ratliff."

"All right, say you and this Les aren't involved. Did you fill him in on all the delicious details of our walk to the river? Did you gloat with him over how you'd wormed your way into the house and within hours had everyone eating out of your hand?"

"No!" So it *was* only his pride that had been crushed. He didn't really care if she had a romantic relationship with Les or not, only if the two of them had made a fool of him. "No," she said softly, shaking her head as she dropped her eyes to stare at the hands she held linked tightly together in her lap.

Lyon gnawed the lining of his mouth. What was it about her that infuriated him so? Why did he give a damn who she talked to on the telephone or what she said? Yet it had wrenched his guts to hear her wishing another man sweet dreams when he knew his own would be haunted by her.

She looked so sad, so contrite. And it could all be a role she was playing. He didn't know if he wanted to strangle her or kiss her. Her mouth promised sweet relief from the bitterness that he tasted each minute of the day. Her breasts intimated surcease from the loneliness he lived with. Her body held the energy that would bring to life what had been dead in him for years.

He had found release for his physical appetites with no small number of compliant females, but each of these interludes had left him feeling empty and tainted. There had been only momentary satisfaction. What he wanted was intimacy with a woman that fully engaged all of the man he was, not just a physical conjunction that gave only fleeting pleasure.

He looked at her again and was surprised to see a tear rolling down her cheek. She looked up at the same time. No, her eyes were dry. That crystal wasn't a tear. It was a raindrop.

"We'd better get back," he said gruffly. "It's starting to rain."

That was an understatement. No sooner had he started the Jeep, than they were deluged by the cloudburst. The rain came down in blinding sheets. "Hold on," he shouted and spun the Jeep around in the opposite direction from the house. He drove pell-mell over the uneven road. His hat was ripped from his head and went sailing off. Andy held on for dear life, the wind tearing at her hair and the rain pelting her face and arms.

He was heading straight for what looked to her like a solid wall of rock. As the cliff rushed toward them she saw the indentation. Lyon pumped the brake, and the Jeep slowed to a crawl that carried it through the mouth of the shallow cave. It was gloomy on the inside, but not ominous. The gloominess was due mostly to the darkness of the sky outside.

Lyon cut the motor, and they were plunged into a heavy silence, broken only by the pounding of the torrent just beyond the entrance of the cave and the slow drip of raindrops off the jeep onto the pebble-floor of the cave.

"Are you all right?" he asked at last.

She was shivering from the cold cloth of her knit top, now clinging damply to her body. From anxiety. From anticipation. "Yes." Her teeth were chattering. Her nipples contracted against the cool air and wet fabric that covered them.

Lyon noticed. He dragged his eyes away. His gaze ricocheted off the walls, ceiling, and floor of the cave, the hood of the car, the back seat, before they came back to her face, which was pale and tense.

He followed the path of a raindrop that rolled from her hairline down her temple, over her cheekbone, and along her jaw until it made a right turn to cling precariously to the tip of her chin. Entirely unplanned, he watched as his index finger reached out and caught it, then withdrew hastily.

Andy sat transfixed.

Lyon turned his head away from her and stared at the rock wall of the cave. His fist lightly thumped his thigh, the only outlet he allowed his inner turmoil. He was like a man holding onto his last few strands of conscience and control, and the knot was slipping.

Then in one swift motion he turned back to her, leaned across the dashboard, and cradled her jaw between his work-roughened palms.

Tilting her head up and back, he raked his thumb along her lower lip. "Please don't be a lie. Please don't be."

His mouth was hot and avid on hers, pushing her lips apart and thrusting his tongue inside. It sank deeply into the warm hollow of her mouth with a purpose so transparent that a groan issued from deep in his chest. Her hands came up to clasp either side of his face, holding his mouth to hers while she met the kiss with heedless fervor.

Finesse and gentleness were forgotten. This was a kiss governed by need, ruled by passion, unplanned, undeniable, and unrestrained—a tidal wave of desire engulfing them both and sweeping them along in a mindless current, a wildfire burning out of control.

They drank of each other thirstily. His tongue teased along the roof of her mouth, her teeth. He compared textures, tasted her, relished what he tasted. The rain had made her skin moist and fragrant with her scent. He abandoned her mouth to bury his face between her throat and chest to breathe and capture it all.

His hands stroked her arms. "Are you cold?"

"No," she sighed. "No." While one hand tugged gently at his earlobe the other was sliding up and down contours of his muscled back.

"Andy, you're not involved with Les Trapper?"

"Only as a co-worker and friend. I'm not involved with anyone. Haven't been since Robert."

He lifted his head to peer at her closely, looking for signs of mendacity lurking in the golden pools of her eyes. "I want to believe you."

"Do. It's true."

"Why do you want to interview my father?"

His question genuinely puzzled her, and her bewilderment showed in her face. "For the reasons I've already told you. Do you think I have some ulterior motive?"

"No. I guess not," he said slowly. "So many have tried for years to invade his privacy. He didn't want the world he had created for himself, my mother, and me to be disrupted. Perhaps if he had consented to give interviews years ago, he wouldn't have been the object of so much speculation.

"The reasons for his reclusiveness are personal. Up until you came he had resolved to go to his grave without ever having to answer a question about himself in order to satisfy the public's curiosity. On the one hand, I'm glad he didn't throw you out." He smiled and ducked his head to kiss her collarbone. Then his eyes grew grave, and he stared fixedly at her earring. "And on the other, I'm afraid for him."

She brushed back a strand of disobedient dark hair that lay damply on his wide forehead. "Why, Lyon?" She gloried in the sound of his name spoken aloud by her own lips and repeated the question just to hear it again. "Because of his health?"

"That and—" His fascination with her earring waned, and he found her eyes much more intriguing. "Never mind." He kissed her. "You're very beautiful, Andy," he murmured against her open lips.

She had experienced a moment of panic as Lyon voiced his private thoughts. Had Les's uncanny ability to sniff out a secret been confirmed again? Was there something about his father that Lyon didn't want known? No! *Please God, don't let me uncover something that would have to be made public*. Conflict of interest was the curse of every reporter who strove for objectivity. She forced the troubling thoughts from her mind and concentrated on the feel of Lyon's lips against hers.

His tongue tickled the corner of her mouth before his lips skimmed along her cheek to play with the earring he had found so interesting before. With one arm clamped firmly around her shoulders, holding her tight, the other hand stroked down her chest. At the upper edge of her top he paused, absorbing the cadence of her heartbeat with his palm.

"Andy?" Permission sought.

"Lyon." Permission granted.

His hand closed over her breast. It was a talented hand, unerringly touching what throbbed with the need to be touched. The damp cloth that clung to her skin only enhanced the friction between his inquisitive fingers and her nerve endings.

"From the moment I saw you sitting on that stool at Gabe's, I wanted to touch you." His whisper in her ear was a caress in itself. "You've been blessed in this department."

"I've always been self-conscious about my size."

He chuckled softly. The exploration continued, became bolder, heightened the tumult building inside her. "You shouldn't be. My adolescence was spent fantasizing about figures like yours."

"And it was fantasizing adolescent boys like you staring at me all the time who made me self-conscious."

"Touché."

"What was your first impression of me when you saw me in Gabe's?"

"That you had gorgeous eyes and a terrific pair of—"

"Besides that!"

"Oh, then you're asking for *second* impressions."

"Lyon, I'm serious."

He laughed. "So am I." Then he did become serious as he lifted his hand from her breast to sift his fingers through her hair, which was still damp with rain. "I thought that you were a very attractive woman whom I would very much like to take to bed."

She swallowed around the knot of emotion in her throat. "And now?"

"Now I think you're a very attractive woman whom I would very much like to get to know better and then take to bed. The first impulse was based solely on lust. The second on something I can't yet put a name to, but the ultimate goal is the same." He held her chin firmly between his thumb and forefinger as his eyes beamed straight into her brain. "Do you understand what I'm saying?"

Tremulously, half-fearfully she said, "I think so."

"I don't want there to be any misunderstanding," he said steadily. How could he be so calm when her entire body was trembling? "I want to make love to you. Slow and leisurely and fast and wildly, in every way conceivable and in some ways inconceivable."

No man had ever had the temerity to talk to her this audaciously, except maybe for Les. But he was always teasing, and Lyon was deadly serious. Embarrassment fired her to respond. "How do you see me? As a trophy for your mantel? A challenge for you to conquer? Guess again, Lyon. I'm not nor ever will be that easily had."

"I didn't mean to suggest that it would be a conquest. I wouldn't want you if you were easily had. I only thought it fair to tell you exactly how I feel. When we do make love, it will be because we both want to, and it will be a mutually satisfying experience."

All the previous encounters of her adult life hadn't prepared her to handle this. She didn't know what to make of this man, her feelings for him, and the things he was saying to her now. Was he only trying to put her off her guard so he could undermine her project? Was that what all this passion was about?

No, he couldn't have pretended that kiss. If he had, he had missed his calling as the world's greatest actor. If he were planning on using sex to stop her from doing the interviews, she'd better set him straight now.

"I'll do my job, Lyon, whatever happens between us. You . . . this has no bearing on why I'm here. I'll never let anything or anyone interfere with my objectivity. I certainly didn't anticipate getting involved with you on any level."

"I didn't exactly foresee my attraction to you either. And I'm still dead set against these interviews."

"You have nothing to fear from me."

"You'll have everything to fear from me if I find out your motives are less than sterling."

On that portentous note he glanced over his shoulder to see that the rain had subsided to a fine drizzle. "We'd better get back. Dad and Gracie will be worried."

Rather than being worried, the two were delighted to see Andy and Lyon stamp through the kitchen door wet to the skin and laughing over the way her feet were slip-sliding in her sandals.

"Since neither of you showed up for lunch, the general ate his here in the kitchen." Gracie mentioned this to explain why Michael Ratliff's wheelchair was occupying one end of the butcher-block table.

"This soup is delicious," he said. "Why don't you two go dry out and then come eat some."

That's what they did, meeting each other at the top of the stairs after they had changed. Andy noted which room was Lyon's and was seized by a feminine curiosity to know what lay behind the door.

"You look like a teenybopper," he said, playfully pulling her wet ponytail. "Well parts of you, anyway." His eyes spoke for him as they dropped to her breasts. "Just for the record, I liked the other top better." She had put on a crisp cotton shirt with rolled-up sleeves and epaulets on the shoulders.

"Lecherous, sexist chauvinists like you would."

His grin was satanic and far too appealing. "Precisely."

His good mood prevailed through the meal they ate in the kitchen, with Gracie and the general for company. When he was finished, Lyon went out, saying that rain didn't stop the work to be done around the ranch. He shrugged on a plastic poncho that was hanging on a hook by the back door and crammed another straw cowboy hat onto his head.

"I'll see everyone at dinner," he said to no one in particular, but he was looking at Andy. Then he winked at her and went out. She made a big production of daintily blotting her mouth with her napkin, but knew that both the general and Gracie had seen Lyon's gesture.

"I'm going to take a short nap, Andy. Then if you want to cover some preliminaries, I'll be at your disposal until dinner."

"That will be fine, general."

"Very good soup, Gracie," he repeated, wheeling out of the room.

"Poor old dear can hardly eat anything. Sometimes the things I have to cook for him make me sick."

Without offering to beforehand and without admonitions that she shouldn't, Andy began helping Gracie clear the table. "He's very ill, isn't he?" she asked quietly, referring to the general.

"Yes, he is," Gracie said bluntly. "I'm trying to prepare

myself, but I know I'll grieve the day he finally departs this earth. He's a great man, Andy."

"I can see that having just met him. You've worked for him for years."

"Almost forty. I was just a girl barely clear of twenty when he and Mrs. Ratliff hired me on. She was a real lady. Delicate as a flower and devoted to him and Lyon. The general never took an interest in women after Rosemary died, though I thought Lyon needed a mother. I think the general subconsciously turned that responsibility over to me."

"Lyon told me that you had taken care of him in place of his mother."

Gracie momentarily stopped sponging off the counter top. "He said that? Then I guess I was successful in mothering him. I worry about that boy. He's got a bitterness eating at him that frightens me."

"He told me that he'd been married."

"To one of the prettiest girls I've ever seen." Gracie sniffed the air as though she were smelling something foul. "Too bad her beauty was only skin deep. She had Lyon dancing on hot coals every day of that doomed marriage. She never gave that boy a day's peace. This was wrong or that was wrong. She whined, complained. Her life was 'wasting away out here in the boondocks.' She needed 'more out of life.'

"She'd always fancied herself being a model or having a career in fashion. So one day she up and hightailed it to New York. Never came back, and as for me and the general we said good riddance. Lyon, though, took it hard. Not so much because he missed her. Frankly I think he was relieved to see her go. But she twisted something on the inside of him."

"He's harboring a great deal of resentment for career women."

Gracie's eloquent brow arched. "You included?"

"Me especially."

"Ah, well, I can see where he might be a bit put out with you for speaking around him the way you did yesterday. Thought it was right clever and humorous myself," she added, laughing. "But you're right. He's suspicious when it comes to women."

"What was her name?"

"Who? His wife? Jerri."

"Jerri," Andy echoed absently.

Gracie assumed the same position from which she had analyzed Andy the day before. Hands crossed over her immense stomach and head tilted to one side, she asked baldly, "Did more happen out there in the rain than just the two of you getting wet?"

Andy felt a wash of color rising to bathe her cheeks. "Ex—excuse me. I've got to go over some notes."

As she awkwardly backed out of the kitchen she heard Gracie chuckle and say, "That's what I thought!"

"So there sat the Wimbledon men's singles winner in my hotel room in London. He was still lugging around that huge trophy with him."

All eyes were turned to Andy as she recounted the story. Even Gracie had stopped serving the after-dinner coffee in order to listen. General Ratliff's eyes were partially closed, but Andy knew he was listening, for he was smiling. Lyon was leaning back in his chair, twirling his wineglass between his thumb and finger.

"As you can imagine I was flattered and thrilled that he had granted me the interview. It was a real coup. The only condition laid down by his coach and manager was that it not take more than ten minutes. You can well imagine how many other media reps were clamoring for a word with him.

"The crew was hustling around, trying to get us lit and wired. Then disaster struck. One of the technicians got overzealous and tripped over the leg of a light tripod. I watched in horror as the light tipped and then began to fall. It was like in a dream when everything is in slow motion, yet there's nothing you can do to prevent the tragedy. The light crashed directly on top of the new Wimbledon champion's head."

Gracie clapped a hand over her mouth. Lyon laughed outright. The general's smile deepened.

"I'm glad you all find it funny," Andy said with feigned indignation. "Though he wasn't seriously hurt, I saw my career flying right out the window."

"What happened?" Lyon asked.

"Since he's not known for his pleasant disposition— quite the contrary in fact—I held my breath. But like a true champion, he carried off the interview with aplomb.

He was dazed for a few moments, but when he recovered, he calmly wiped the blood—"

"Blood!" Gracie shrieked.

"Didn't I mention the blood?" Andy asked innocently. Then they all laughed. "Truthfully he wasn't harmed, but as that light was falling, I could just see the head-lines: WIMBLEDON CHAMPION DIES AT HANDS OF AMERICAN JOURNALIST."

"Who else have you interviewed?" Gracie asked, breaking with tradition and sitting down at the dining table, not even pretending any longer to be serving.

"Let's see," Andy said musingly. "Some have been the greats and near greats, others just plain folks who for one reason or another found themselves in the news."

"Name some of the greats," the housekeeper urged her.

Andy cast a concerned eye toward Michael Ratliff, but he seemed to be relaxed and not overly tired. They had talked for a long while that afternoon, him providing her with dates and pertinent information that would help her during the interviews ahead. "Bob Hope, Neil Armstrong, Reggie Jackson, John Denver, Prince Andrew of England, Mikhail Baryshnikov."

"Ahhhh," Gracie said in awe.

"All men?" Lyon asked peevishly.

"No." Andy smiled. "There's also been Lauren Bacall, Judge Sandra Day O'Connor, Carol Burnett, Farrah Fawcett, and Diana Ross. To name just a few," she added mischievously as she ticked the names off on her fingers.

"Whom would you like to interview that you haven't?" Lyon asked.

"General Michael Ratliff," she said smiling, and he raised his hand like a pontiff blessing the multitude. "And"—she rolled her eyes heavenward—"Robert Redford."

Gracie hooted. "Now you're talking."

The general laughed out loud. "I'm glad to be in such august company."

Lyon, too, was laughing, and Andy loved the wholesome, rumbling sound of it. "Dad," he said when they had all calmed down, "you'd better get to bed."

"You're right, of course, though I hardly noticed I was tired. The company was so charming and entertaining." Andy went over to him as she had done before and kissed him on the cheek.

"Good night. Get some rest."

"Good night." He left the dining room in his wheelchair.

Lyon asked Gracie, "Did the doctor come this morning?"

"Yes, while you were caught in the rain."

"And?"

She placed a comforting hand on his shoulder. "It's in the Lord's hands, Lyon."

He reached over and patted her hand and looked up at her solemnly. After a moment he shook his head to ward off the gloomy subject and stood up. "Andy, I hate to desert you, but I've got a Cattlemen's Association meeting tonight. Will you be all right?"

Flooded with disappointment, she smiled bravely. "Certainly. I need to study anyway."

"Good night then."

"Good night." It was long after she heard the front door closing behind him that she could take the initiative and leave the dining room.

She never was sure what awakened her. Just suddenly she was awake and sitting up in her bed. The clock on the bedside table indicated with its glowing hands that it was after four o' clock. She threw off the covers and padded to the window, for some reason exercising stealth.

Everything was still. Then she heard a noise. Poised to listen, she thought it was coming from the direction of the river. Her heart sprang to her throat when she saw the bobbing flashlights slashing through the darkness. Two lights, moving erratically through the trees. First one was extinguished, then another.

Who could it be? Ranch hands? She glanced toward the bunkhouse. All was quiet. Intruders? But who? Could other reporters have learned she was here and come to investigate for themselves?

No matter who it was, Lyon had to know.

Racing across the bedroom, she flung open the door and flew down the hallway. Not even pausing to knock, she turned the knob of Lyon's door and pushed it open. Allowing only a second for her eyes to adjust to the darkness of his room where no moonlight penetrated, she crept toward the massive bed against the adjacent wall.

He was lying on his stomach. His arm was draped over the pillow. His nose was buried in the crook of his elbow. His bare back was broad and dark against the sheets. Leaning over him, she touched his shoulder lightly.

"Lyon."

Chapter Five

❧

He jerked upright, nearly bumping her chin with his head. Rapidly blinking eyes focused on her. "What . . .? Andy? What?"

"There's something going on down by the river," she said, the words stumbling out of her mouth. She didn't know if her heart was thudding because of the possibility of danger, or because she was being treated to a close-up view of Lyon's bare chest. "Flashlights, some kind of noise."

He slung his legs over the edge of the bed. "The river?"

"Yes. I woke up and—"

She broke off when he stood up. He was naked. He brushed past her in the dark, for an instant the hair on his chest whispering against her arm. He grabbed a pair of jeans that were folded over a valet and pulled them on.

"What kind of noise?" His jeans were the western type with buttons on the fly. He was working at them.

"Uh . . ." Andy stammered. "Uh, like laughter, sort of . . ." She trailed off lamely as the snap at the top of his jeans cracked loudly in the still house.

"How many flashlights?" He went to a bureau and opened the top drawer.

"Two I think. What do you think—Is that a *gun*?"

"Yes. Thanks for waking me. It's probably nothing, but I'd better investigate." He pushed the gun into the waistband of his jeans and reached back in the drawer for a flashlight.

"I'm going, too."

"Like hell."

"I'm going, and if I don't go with you, I'll just follow."

He stopped at the door, turning around to face her. Even in the darkness—they knew better than to turn on any lights and alert whoever was down by the river—he could see the stubborn set of her chin.

"Come on, then," he said with no small amount of exasperation. She followed his stalking shadow down the hallway to the stairs. They made it to the back door without mishap and apparently without waking anyone else. "Stay close," he whispered as he opened one of the sliding glass doors leading out to the pool and terrace.

Moving like cat burglars, they crossed the patio, skirted the pool, and then took the paved path toward the river. Once they had gained the path, Lyon glanced over his shoulder at her. "Still there?"

"Yes."

He stumbled in the dark when he caught sight of the apparition trailing behind him. "What in the hell do you have on?"

"A nightgown."

"A very white nightgown. You look like Lady Macbeth. Anyone will be able to see you from a mile off. Anything under it?"

"Panties."

"Thank God," he grumbled. "Damn!" he cursed suddenly and viciously. "Do you have on any shoes?" he hissed.

"No."

"Then be careful of rocks."

She giggled.

Midway down the path Lyon came to an abrupt halt. Andy ran into him from behind. It seemed only natural that she leave her hands at his waist, where they had reflexively come to rest in an attempt to break her fall. "There's a light," he said softly.

The beam of the flashlight darted through the trees like a drunken firefly. The rushing river water masked most other sound, but there was the undeniable murmur of voices. One of them emphasized a word and there followed a chorus of *shhhh*.

"Step easy," Lyon said, taking steps forward. Her feet bumped into his as she scooted along behind him, still holding on to the waistband of his jeans.

Through the dense lower branches of the trees they could see several dark figures silhouetted against the moonlit sky and the river, which looked like liquid silver. The figures moved awkwardly, tripping over rocks and nature's litter beneath the trees. Someone cursed under his breath. There followed a series of smothered giggles. Andy was relieved by the intruders' bungling. They couldn't be professional criminals of any kind.

"Well I'll be damned," Lyon said in a soft whisper. He turned toward her. "We're going to have some fun. Play along."

"But what—"

"Just play along. You'll see."

He made a noise like stampeding elephants as he thrashed through the last few trees that separated them from the riverbank. Andy jumped when he roared out, "What in hell is going on here?" Only then did he turn on his super-beamed flashlight. She saw one or two of the trespassers scurry for cover in a large rubber raft she hadn't noticed until it was illuminated by Lyon's light.

Three men, about eighteen years old, stood like animals paralyzed by the beams of headlights along the highway, frozen in terror as Lyon bore down on them with gun drawn and light blazing. He came to within a few feet of the first figure, who slowly raised himself up from a self-protective crouch. "You're not going to shoot us or anything, are you?"

"I don't know yet," Lyon said threateningly. "Who are you and what are you doing sneaking around on my property in the middle of the night?"

The young man cast an anxious glance over his shoulder, seeking reinforcement, but his cronies hung back. Something in the raft moved with a rustling noise. "We . . . we're students at UT. We were rafting down the river. The guy where we rented the raft said you ranchers didn't mind us riding past your places if we didn't pull in."

"Well?" Lyon said, impatiently shifting his weight from one foot to the other and hefting the gun in his hand. "You pulled in."

The culprit swallowed visibly. "We . . . uh, got to drinking beer and uh . . . sort of overturned the raft when we were coming through those rapids a few yards upstream. We just pulled in here to wring everything out and re-group. So to speak."

Another muffled giggle from the raft caused him to glance furtively over his shoulder. He faced Lyon again with trepidation. "We're awfully sorry, sir. We didn't mean to do anything. Swear to God we didn't."

Lyon, seemingly with some reluctance, put the gun back in his waistband and the young man's shoulders slumped in relief, as did those of his friends. Placing an arm around her shoulders, Lyon pulled Andy around him to his side.

"You nearly frightened my wife to death. We had just been making love when she went to the window and saw your flashlights down here. She thought it was her ex-husband coming for his revenge. He's in an institution for the criminally insane and prone to acts of violence."

Andy stared at him with mute dismay, but she was having a hard time keeping a straight face. For the reference to their making love, which had caused six eighteen-year-old eyes to turn to her with lascivious interest, she ground her heel over Lyon's big toe. Other than a tensing of the muscles in his jaw, he showed no reaction.

"We're sure sorry we disturbed you while . . . I mean, we didn't mean to interrupt your . . . we're sorry we bothered you," the spokesman for the dripping group finally managed to get out.

"Andy, go check to see if those silly girls hiding in the raft are unharmed and not being held there against their will."

"No, sir, they're not. They're just scared."

Sparing her bare feet from the bruising rocks and twigs, Andy tiptoed over to the raft and peered inside. Three girls were huddled together. Their hair and clothes were soaked. They looked at her with chagrin as they began to unfold and step out of the rubber raft. After a cursory glance it looked to Andy as though the only provisions brought along for the trip were six-packs of beer. "Are you all right?" she asked the disheveled trio.

"Yes, ma'am," they said in unison, and Andy marveled at the sudden show of manners. They probably hadn't said "ma'am" since the first grade.

"Is there any more beer in there, Andy?" Lyon asked.

"Yes."

He came over and picked up two of the six-packs and handed one to her. She held it with one hand while trying to hold her nightgown closer to her body with the other. In the moonlight she knew her figure was clearly outlined through the sheer fabric.

"It'll be dawn in about an hour," Lyon was saying. "If I see you after that, I'll come back. If I see one scrap of paper, one cigarette butt, any litter you might have left behind, I'll call the sheriff and have you arrested on sight for trespassing. Is that understood?"

Andy would have answered in the affirmative to any order given in that tone of voice. He had inherited his ability to inspire obedience from his father.

"Yes, sir." Lyon waited until all six had responded.

"All right, then. And from now on, to save yourself possible injury, I'd suggest you wait until you put in for the night before you break out the beer. This river can be dangerous and it's totally irresponsible to drink while you're trying to navigate it."

"Yes, sir." Another meek chorus.

"Come on, Andy, we can go back to bed now."

She shot him a murderous look before she preceded him up the path to the house. The voices behind them were subdued as the group began gathering the things they had dragged out of the raft. If the dousing in the river hadn't them up, Lyon certainly had.

"I'm going to kill you," she said over her shoulder as she huffed up the gentle incline.

"Why?" he asked innocently.

"*Wife?* With an insane ex-husband no less. Where did you come up with that?"

"Would you rather I'd said, 'This is my houseguest, Ms. Malone'? What conclusions do you think they'd have drawn if I'd introduced you like that? Especially with you traipsing around with me in the great outdoors half-naked in the middle of the night?"

"I was *traipsing* around in the middle of the night because I thought all of us might be in danger. And I'm not half-naked."

"Virtually naked."

"That's better." They laughed softly. "But you didn't have to tell them that we'd been . . . uh . . ."

"Making love?"

"Yes," she said, glad that her back was to him. Every once in a while she'd feel the heat of his body as he walked close behind her. "You could have said that we were sleeping."

"Yes, but something so mundane wouldn't have gotten their attention nearly as well. They were stupefied at the sight of you anyway."

"Their stupefaction was due to your light and the gun."

"Actually it's a pistol," he corrected. "Maybe at first they were concentrating only on that, but I saw their roving eyes. If I hadn't said you were my wife and if I hadn't intimated that we were very happily married, they might have been tempted to overpower me and take you."

"Don't forget the girls they had with them."

"Who looked like three drowned rats. No, I think they would have preferred you." They were at the back door now, and he was depositing the confiscated beer on one of the patio tables. "You look good, you know, tousled from bed and virtually naked."

She slipped past him through the door as he stepped aside. "Thank you," she mumbled. Thank you? What was she doing saying thank you when she should have slapped his face?

"For an instant," he said on a whisper, "after you woke me up, I thought that maybe you had come to my room for another reason."

She stumbled on the first few stairs and her gracelessness had nothing to do with the floor-length hem of her nightgown. Not deigning to recognize the suggestiveness of what he'd said, she asked, "How long had you been asleep? What time did you get home?"

"About eleven thirty. Some of us went out for a drink after the meeting."

Some? Who? Women? He must surely never be long without a woman. "I read for a while, boning up for tomorrow. Then about eleven I went to sleep. I didn't hear you when you came in."

"Oh." He sounded disappointed. "How did you hear our night prowlers?"

They were at her door now. She leaned against the jamb. "I don't know. I just woke up suddenly, knowing instinctively that something wasn't right."

"You weren't really frightened, were you?"

"Not until you started packing heat! I wasn't frightened until you got that gun."

"Pistol."

"Pistol. And did they think we wouldn't hear those girls giggling?"

Lyon's shoulders shook with silent laughter. "We scared the hell out of them."

"Does that happen often? People rafting on the river, I mean."

He took the pistol out of his waistband and set it with the flashlight on a credenza in the hall. He propped one shoulder against the wall.

"Frequently during the spring and summer. There are rapids all along the Guadalupe. People rent rafts, usually for the day. Most of the trips only take several hours. But some require spending the night on the river. Of course, the rafters have to camp on public grounds and not private property. We get waved at occasionally as they drift by. That's all. The Guadalupe only makes one loop through a corner of our property."

She loved listening to the lulling sound of his voice. It occurred to her that for an hour they had forgotten their antipathy. They had laughed, shared a memorable experience, and the hostility between them had given way to companionship. She grieved for what could have been had they met under different circumstances. He wouldn't have been suspicious of her motives. She wouldn't have looked upon him as an obstacle, an enemy, but only as a man.

The sky was turning gray with the encroaching dawn, and the darkness of the hallway had been gradually dispelled enough for her to see his features clearly. Relaxed now, his mouth lacked the hardness that often drew it taut. The laugh lines around his eyes were more evident when he smiled. White against the dark tan of his face, they etched a fine network she'd love to track with her finger. The muscles in his arms bulged as he crossed them over his chest, the broad chest that was so alluringly furred with dark hair.

"Will you go back to sleep?" he asked softly.

Was he looking at her mouth? "No. Probably not. I'd only get a headache if I dozed off and then had to wake up shortly. You?"

He dragged his unwilling eyes upward until they met hers. "Uh, no. I usually get up around dawn anyway."

She nodded, looked down the length of the hallway, at the floor, at her bare feet positioned so close to his. She had been with him for over an hour wearing nothing more than a wisp of a nightgown and a scanty pair of underwear. Only now, in the quiet of the predawn house, was she self-conscious about her flimsy attire. "Well, thanks for the adventure," she said lightly, though her throat felt heavy. Her whole body felt heavy, laden with need.

"My pleasure. I'll see you later."

"Yes."

There was nothing else to say except maybe "Why don't you come in?" or "We could continue this discussion in my room," or "I ache for you. Please kiss me." But she could say none of those things. Rather than say anything else that would be superfluous, she went through the oak door and softly closed it behind her.

She listened for his footsteps, but after a moment remembered that he was barefoot and finally left her post at the door. At loose ends and not knowing quite what to do, she decided she'd shower and wash her hair now. Then she'd used the remaining time until the crew arrived to study her notes.

The water felt delightful, and she was refreshed and wide awake afterward. Not that she'd needed anything to revive her. Every sensory impression was heightened. Her nerves tingled. She was aware of each one as she dried herself, applied a citrusy after-bath splash, and smoothed lotion on her arms and legs.

She hadn't brought any underwear into the bathroom, so she slipped the batiste nightgown back on. The soft, thin cotton settled around her like a cloud. Scoop-necked and held on by two thin spaghetti straps, it coolly caressed her clean body.

Returning to the bedroom, she sat in the window seat to dry her hair. Since it seemed to have a mind of its own, she had given up years ago trying to make it conform to a rigid style. Now, as it dried, she wielded a hairbrush like an animal trainer does a whip, never totally successful in taming the beast. To her amusement she was often asked where she had her hair done.

The sun broke over the farthest hill and poured a golden pink glow over the landscape. It was a breathtaking sight, pastoral and peaceful. Lyon's love for his land was understandable and justified.

A tentative tap on her door distracted her from the view. "Yes?"

Taking that as assent, Lyon opened the door, holding a tray aloft. "I made some coffee and thought you . . ."

He'd never seen anything more beautiful nor remembered ever wanting a woman more. Her arm was curved over her head, holding the hairbrush where it had been when he surprised her by opening the door. The honey-colored hair swirled around her head like a halo, reflecting the new sun. Her skin looked translucent in the soft light. Beneath the nightgown her dusky nipples were promising shadows that peaked temptingly against the cloth.

The tray was set down and forgotten on a small table. Lyon shut the door and crossed the room, his eyes never leaving her, compelling her not to move, not to speak. He'd never felt this way in his life. From adolescence he'd known his way around the female anatomy, and he'd never lacked for partners to practice what knowledge he possessed.

For a while after Jerri left, he hadn't been kind, but had approached each woman selfishly, never caring about her, only wanting what he felt was owed to him because of the humiliation he'd suffered at the hands of his wife. That attitude had mellowed considerably, and any woman who had known his love, for the brief time he alloted her, would never forget his touch. His masculine pride had been restored.

Now he felt as callow as a boy. He only hoped Andy couldn't sense his susceptibility as he came to the window seat and sat down beside her where she was curled in the corner.

"I didn't mean to disturb you." Always raspy, his voice was even huskier now.

"You didn't."

He embraced her first with his eyes. The gray irises that she had seen hardened and as cold as steel were now warm with emotion as he studied her face. Each feature was catalogued before his eyes surveyed her throat and the smooth expanse of her chest. In no respect did he find her wanting.

"You smell good."

"I just took a shower."

Their inane conversation was only an outlet for the tension that shackled them both, an excuse to release some of the excess energy that had welled up inside them, a reason to expel the breath that had become trapped in shrinking lungs.

He touched her hair, threading his fingers through it and then combing it outward until each strand had drifted through them to settle once again on her shoulders.

His fingers ghosted over her face, touching brow, eyelids, nose, cheekbones. Her lips were smoothed by alternating index fingers until he had them memorized by shape and texture. Certainly by color. Hopefully by taste.

She wanted him to kiss her then, but he didn't. His hands continued on their wandering down her neck, across her collarbone, detailing the hollow between it and her shoulder with a playful finger. Then he arrived at the piping that outlined the neckline of her gown.

He looked deeply into her eyes hypnotically, and like an obedient subject she closed them. He brushed his fingers across her nipples, fanning them gently. He was instantaneously rewarded with their pouting response.

"Andy," he breathed. He hooked his thumbs under the thin straps, and the nightgown was drawn down to frothily encircle her waist. She lifted her arms free and placed her hands around his neck, stroking his jawline with her thumbs.

He looked at her breasts. From beneath he cupped her and lifted her slightly. Gently his thumbs stroked the peachy crests. "You've never had a baby?" he asked gruffly.

"No." She responded in kind.

"Why?"

"My husband didn't want one." She didn't want to say Robert's name, didn't want a third party to intrude on this occasion.

"What a waste." He lowered his head and kissed the lush top curve, then inched his lips down, dropping damp kisses that cooled against her warm skin, until his lips skated over the nipple. Andy heard her own whimper of need. He heard it, too, and his mouth opened over her. With a sweet urgent tugging she was enveloped by his mouth. His tongue nudged her with the most erotic caress she'd ever experienced.

"Lyon." His name was half sigh, half ecstatic cry, and she grasped his head between her hands and held him fast.

"You taste like thick, sweet cream," he murmured as his mouth glided from one breast to the other. His ardent

111

attention continued until her nerves were quivering like harp strings.

Lifting his head, he saw that his mouth had added a glossiness to her already glowing skin. He smiled. His arms went around her and drew her closer, until, as they both watched, the tips of her breasts pressed into the curling mat on his chest.

Lifting their eyes, aware that their heartbeats were resonating with each other, they smiled. "You're cream and"—he lowered his lips to hers—"honey."

His mouth fastened on hers possessively and cohesively. His tongue scoured her mouth repeatedly as though he truly were gathering honey.

She strained upward and forward until she was molded to him as closely as their bodies would allow. Not believing that skin could feel so satiny, time and again his palms made the journey from her shoulder to her waist. For heart-stopping moments his hands lingered at that curving indentation. Then, emboldened, they slipped below the nightgown gathered at her waist and cradled her hips, lifting her up.

Together they stood. The nightgown floated unheeded to the floor. He lifted her free of it as he picked her up and carried her into the deeper shadows of the room, where the unmade bed was an open invitation.

He lay her down and followed with his own body. It was heavy and hard and rough compared to her soft smoothness. She loved it, yet she fought the explosive desire that flooded her. "This is wrong, Lyon."

"God, don't you think I know that?" He kissed her hungrily. Impatiently he groped for the buttons on his jeans. He tore his mouth free. "But do you want to stop it? *Can* you stop it?"

His hands roved over her flesh, finding erogenous places she didn't know were there. *No, I can't stop it*, she thought vaguely with what mental capacity was left to her. She surrendered to the intuitive caresses of his hands that swirled her into a maelstrom of longing. "We didn't plan it, did we?" she asked, arching against him. "We didn't . . . ah, Lyon, Lyon."

He lifted his head only long enough to look at what he touched. "Soft. So soft. Such a golden girl," he whispered hoarsely. "A beautiful golden girl."

It was tormenting to wait while he grappled again with the fly on the jeans. They were laughing quietly about their shared frustration when an insistent tapping rattled the door.

The laughter broke off abruptly and all motion on the bed ceased.

"Andy?" Gracie's voice was muffled—fortunately the panels of the door were thick. "Andy, are you awake yet, honey?"

Andy cleared her throat and tried to sound as though she had just been awakened. "Yes, Gracie. What is it?" Her eyes never left Lyon's as he remained poised above her. His chest expanded like a bellows with his uneven, harsh breathing.

"Your boys are here. Four of them just arrived in a van.

I've given them coffee and told them to wait for you downstairs."

Lyon's soft, but expansive curse scorched her ears. "I'll be down shortly," Andy said.

"Take your time," Gracie called back. "I'll feed them breakfast."

"Thank you," Andy said miserably.

For long moments neither of them moved, then Lyon eased away from her. He levered himself off the bed and deftly fastened the buttons that had been so contrary only moments ago. Andy reached for the sheet to cover herself.

"Modesty at this late date, Ms. Malone?"

His sarcasm banished any lingering passion or regret over their being interrupted. "No." Disdaining the sheet, she jumped off the bed, walked across the bedroom, and pulled on a light robe.

He eyed her with derision. "So you *are* ashamed."

She faced him defensively. "All right. Yes! Yes, I am. I should never have let you touch me."

"I thought as much," he said scornfully. "You'd hate to be accused of consorting with the enemy. Or are you afraid Les will find out about your close call with dalliance?"

"I've told you that Les and I—Oh, it doesn't matter. You're only going to believe what you've already made up your mind to. Why are you angry with me? I'm no more to blame than you are. I didn't know the crew would arrive at just this moment. Do you think I arranged this to humiliate you?"

"I think that you, Ms. Malone, are relieved that you were rescued in the nick of time."

"I think you are, too," she flung back.

"Damn right. This was the height of stupidity," he said, slamming the fist of one hand into the opposite palm. "I knew better, *know* better, than to . . ."

He paced, talking to himself, not to her, but each word was like a wound in her heart. He whirled around to face her again. "Why do you have to look like a damn goddess if you're untouchable? Huh?" His anger was fearsome, and she shrank from it. "You've driven me crazy since the first time I laid eyes on you, but stay away from me from now on."

"What!" she exclaimed, pushing away from the security of the wall where she had been cowering. Her fists ground into her hips. "*Me*? Stay away from *you*? How dare you insinuate that I initiated this. I didn't exactly chase you around this bedroom this morning."

"No, but you came sneaking into mine in the middle of the night wearing a sorry excuse for a nightgown."

"You were naked!"

"In my own bed. I didn't come creeping into your room that way."

"I only came creeping into yours because I thought we, especially your father, could be in danger. If not us personally, then your property. Forgive me for warning you!" she shouted.

"You could have put on that robe a little sooner!" he shouted back.

"In the rush I didn't think of it."

"Well, think about it next time."

"There won't be one."

"You've got that right. You stay out of my way, and I'll stay out of yours."

"Fine!" she screamed, but she didn't think he'd heard her. He'd already slammed out the door.

She stood in the middle of the room for several minutes, staring at the door, pressing balled hands to her lips. Gulping at air that seemed to have been vacuumed out of the room with Lyon's angry exit, she wondered how she was going to explain her tear-reddened eyes to her crew.

Chapter Six

T he crew greeted her warmly when she joined them in the kitchen a good half-hour after Gracie had knocked on her door. It had taken her that long to recover from the verbal blows Lyon had dealt her.

"Sorry," she said, hugging each of them in turn, "but I had something in my eye that took forever to get out." It was possible, though highly implausible, but they seemed to accept the explanation for her red, swollen eyes. "Think you can camouflage them on camera, Jeff?"

"You're so gorgeous, who'd notice a couple of bloodshot eyes?"

Lyon chose that moment to push open the swinging door. Stiffly, but trying to act normally lest she alert the crew to the undercurrents between Lyon and her, she introduced him around.

"This is Jeff, our cinematographer." Andy hadn't taken Jeff's comment seriously about her being gorgeous. He was a notorious flirt, and his camera was his license to get away with it. He used the mystique attached to a motion-picture camera to its full extent. Andy felt sorry for his pretty, meek wife, who waited patiently at home while he went out on frequent assignments. Jeff had never passed up an opportunity to be unfaithful, but early on Andy had let him know she wasn't interested. His flirting with her was all for show.

She wondered if people had pitied her when Robert was away in the same way she did Jeff's wife. More than likely they had. During the last year of their marriage Robert hadn't been satisfied with the romantic aspects of it and had sought consolation elsewhere.

"Jeff," Lyon said, shaking the photographer's hand. "Lyon Ratliff."

"This is Gil, our sound man."

"Mr. Ratliff." Gil shook Lyon's hand deferentially. He was a likable guy who offended no one and did his job so well he was often ignored. His self-effacing personality had endeared him to Andy, and she could ask for the moon and he'd try to get it for her.

"Tony does our lighting." Andy presented him to Lyon. Tony was often querulous, probably because he had six children to clothe and feed. But he was a master at highlighting, shading, and filtering.

The last crew member was a PA — production assistant. To him fell the jobs that had to be done and which no one else had any time or desire to do. Warren, a skeletal frame with skin stretched over it, had the strength of an ox and the agility of a monkey. He had been known to climb trees, ford rivers, tunnel through brush, or dangle from perilous perches to help the specialists get just the picture or sound they wanted.

"I see that Gracie's already given you breakfast," Lyon said, and the four groaned. He laughed. "Probably more than you bargained for."

Andy was amazed at his geniality. Was she the one who would have to bear the brunt of his hostility?

"Make yourselves at home. When the time comes, Gracie will telephone the bunkhouse and someone will take you down there. If you need anything, tell Ms. Malone, and she'll notify me."

Ms. Malone.

The crew, even Jeff, seemed impressed with Lyon Ratliff, and Andy felt betrayed. She resented the hospitality and graciousness he had extended to them. When he went out the door, looking smugly satisfied, she knew he'd been deliberately effusive. It was his way of telling her that he could be nice when he wanted to be, but that he didn't want to be nice to her. Her jaws began to ache before she realized how tightly she was clenching her teeth.

The first disaster occurred when Gil discovered that one of his microphone cords had gone dead. "I don't know what's wrong with it, Jeff," he said placidly when the temperamental photographer lit into him. "It's just not drawing power."

"Gil, do you think you can find one here in Kerrville?" Andy asked in the voice of a mediator.

"I don't know. I can try. If not, I'll have to go to San Antonio."

Andy ignored Jeff's muttered cursing.

"Then take the van. While you're gone, we'll set up for the first shoot. As soon as you return, we'll start."

Eventually everything worked out well, though Andy's concern was never for the crew, but for the general. Dressed in a suit and tie, he had been ready to start the interviews that morning, as Andy had told him they would. She had felt that the earlier they started, the better. That would give him the afternoons and evenings to rest before the session the following day. The project would take longer doing just one program a day, but she had promised herself, not to mention Lyon, that she would do everything she could to protect the general from fatigue.

She was disappointed that he hadn't worn his army uniform, but when she tentatively suggested that he might consider it, he became visibly flustered.

"I never ordered another one after I retired. The ones I have are moth-eaten and forty years old. I'd rather not, thanks."

She was puzzled and let down, but she smiled and touched him on the shoulder. "If you'd rather not, that's fine. Besides, if you looked any more handsome, I might not be able to keep my mind on the questions."

Gil returned while they were eating the sandwiches Gracie had fixed them for lunch. While he was setting up, Andy went upstairs to put on her "camera" makeup, pull her hair into its soft bun, and dress in an ivory linen dress, with no jewelry except for pearl earrings.

She received the usual wolf whistles from the crew as she descended the stairs with her notes in her hand. She bowed to them like a grand dame of the theater and did a slow pirouette. As she turned around she came face to face with Lyon, who had been watching her clowning with a face carved of stone and condemning eyes.

"I see that you're in your element, Ms. Malone." The judgmental tone of his voice irritated her more than nails on a chalkboard. She took the bait.

"Yes, I am."

"Good. I'd hate for you to lose your knack."

"So would I, Mr. Ratliff."

"You'd never let that happen, would you?"

"Not on your life," she said defiantly.

His voice dropped considerably. "It's *your* life we're talking about." He looked at her with uncompromising disapproval, then went to his father to check on him.

General Michael Ratliff was sitting regally in an armchair in the living room. He was wired for sound, though Gil had carefully concealed all the cords. Only the small lavalier mike peeked from behind his necktie. Andy was gratified to see that her crew treated him with the utmost respect.

She took her place at the end of the sofa next to his chair, and allowed Gil to attach her microphone to a discreet spot on her bodice. Out of the corner of her eye she saw Lyon watching closely as Gil's hands fiddled with the fabric over her breast. She'd seen less menacing expressions on the faces of offended despots.

"A little more cheek color," Jeff said impersonally as he eyed her through his lens. "Why haven't you taken advantage of the Texas sun, Andy? You look pale."

"It rained yesterday," she said absently as Warren scrambled to bring her the makeup kit she had brought from upstairs. Her eyes involuntarily sought out Lyon's, and for a moment they stared at each other over the equipment that had converted a comfortable living room into a television studio. She forced her eyes away, and the mirror in her hands was shaking as she applied more blusher to her cheeks.

"There's a glare on General Ratliff's face," Jeff said.

Warren adjusted a drape over the window.

"Ooookaaaay, everybody's lookin' good. Ready when you are, Andy," Jeff said. "Gil, got your mike levels?"

"Yep. Sounds good."

"Okay. Andy?"

"Ready," she said licking her lips.

"And we're rollin'."

She stumbled once during her introductory remarks and they had to start over. What she had done hundreds of times before was now making her incredibly nervous. Actually it wasn't so incredible. Lyon. If she had not known he was in the room, listening to every word and weighing it, watching each gesture and criticizing it, she would have been perfectly at ease.

Michael Ratliff was an excellent interview subject. He answered her questions expansively, expounding on them without any prodding on her part. Her personal philosophy when it came to interviewing was to get the subject to talk openly, asking him as few questions as possible. She felt it was the subject, not her, the audience wanted to see and hear. Andy Malone was only the usher who escorted the celebrity into their living rooms.

For the first interview she limited her questions to the general's personal history, his childhood, his education, his early years in the army.

"You aren't a native Texan, though you've lived here since your retirement."

"No, I was born in Missouri and grew up there. My father was an iceman." He related a few anecdotes about his parents and his one brother, who had died during the thirties.

"How is it that you came to retire in Texas?"

"Well, I'll tell you about that, Andy." He was totally unaffected by the camera and talked to her as though they were alone. It was her own disregard for the camera once it started rolling that put her interviewees so much at ease. She took the subtle time cues from Warren with barely a blink of her eyes. The subject never noticed.

The general told a story about how he had first come to the hill country of Texas with a friend to hunt elk. He fell in love with the limestone-dotted hills and lovely rivers fed by underground springs, and decided that he would settle there after his retirement.

"And did you get an elk?"

He laughed. "No. I never could shoot worth a damn. You can ask my son, Lyon. I never made higher than marksman in the Army. My contemporaries teased me about it unmercifully—they said that if the soldiers under my command hadn't been able to shoot any better than their general, we'd have never won the war."

On that note Andy concluded the first interview.

"Terrific!" Jeff said, switching off his camera and unlatching it from its tripod.

Lyon started pushing the wheelchair through the maze of lights and cable. "We'll need him for about five minutes more, Lyon," Andy said. "We have to do reverse questions."

"What's that?"

She explained that when only one camera was being used, after the interview the photographer would move his equipment over behind the subject, this time focusing on her. She would repeat some of the questions she had asked, but the general wouldn't respond, only sit still. Then an editor would mix the two segments of tape, first showing Andy asking the question, then the general as he was answering it in the real interview.

"It's a trick to make it seem like we had more than one camera. The transitions are edited so smoothly that the audience never notices they're there."

The general took his directions from Jeff, who was holding the camera on his shoulder and focusing on Andy past the general's head.

"Dad, are you all right?"

"Yes, son. I haven't had this much fun and excitement in a long time. During the war whenever I was interviewed, there were swarming reporters with flash cameras in their hands. Every once in a while I did a radio interview, but this is different."

Andy was glad he was enjoying himself, but she didn't like the high color in his cheeks any more than Lyon did. She did the reverse questions flawlessly and quickly. They were finished within a matter of minutes. Tony switched off the hot lights.

"You're a true pro, sweetheart," Jeff enthused, hugging her tight and kissing her smackingly on the cheek. Gil had gently separated the general from his microphone and was now unhooking hers, taking care not to snag her dress. Lyon was assisting his father into the wheelchair, but hadn't missed Jeff's show of affection. His eyes were hard as they drilled into her.

Out of regard for the general's health the crew had refrained from smoking. Now they all filed out the front door to take in their required ration of nicotine.

Andy knelt in front of General Ratliff's chair. She looked up into the lined, age-spotted face. "Thank you. You were wonderful."

"I enjoyed it. I thought perhaps you'd change personalities when the camera came on, that you'd become hard, curt, and demanding. I should have known you'd remain the gracious lady that you are."

She stood up to kiss him on the cheek. "You'd better rest. We'll be at it again tomorrow."

Since they had gotten a late start, it was almost dinnertime by the time they secured the equipment for the night. As with most cinematographers, Jeff treated his camera like a baby and coddled it lovingly. Tony's lights were safely restored to their metal boxes. Gil's microphones were replaced in their cushioned cases.

They were like ten-year-old boys over the idea of sharing their quarters with real cowboys and hastened down to the bunkhouse to take their evening meal. The general ate off a tray in the seclusion of his bedroom. Andy had to endure a virtually silent meal alone with Lyon.

"Are you satisfied with how the interview went today?" he asked. They were well into the main course before he broke the oppressive, unnerving silence.

"Yes. Your father is a natural before the camera. Often we have to remind the interviewee that he's talking to me and not to the camera. They want to look at it instinctively. But your father was oblivious to the camera and the lights. He was an interviewer's dream."

"Your crew seem to like you."

Andy knew there was more to the statement than a surface observation. "We've worked well together for years. Sometimes I'm assigned other technicians. It's not always the same ones, though this team is my favorite. They're very professional."

"Um-huh."

Water sloshed out of her glass when she slammed it down onto the linen-covered table. "What's that supposed to mean?"

"What?" he asked innocently.

"That 'um-huh' that drips with implication."

"I meant to imply nothing," he said, with so much feigned sincerity she wanted to scream. "If you read anything into my 'um-huh,' then it's your guilty conscience that's doing it."

"I don't have a guilty conscience!"

"Then why are you shouting?" he asked with a serenity that infuriated her.

"Tell Gracie I'll skip dessert tonight," she said, shoving her chair away from the table.

At the door his lilting voice reached her. "Sweet dreams, Andy."

The mocking repetition of what he had heard her say to Les released the anger raging inside her. She spun around. "Go to hell, Lyon," she said in a sugary voice. Then she stormed from the room.

The next day went smoothly, with only minor crises cropping up that were quickly dealt with. The crew was suffering from hangovers brought on by too many long-neck bottles of Lone Star beer, but Andy was unsympathetic and unconcerned. She'd seen them do some of their best work after a night of revelry.

General Ratliff was as relaxed and loquacious as he'd been the day before. This time the interview took place in the garden room where she'd first met him. Jeff taped it using the natural sunlight, asking Tony to fill in with light only where absolutely necessary. He even left the ceiling fan on, to gently stir Andy's hair and the leafy plants behind her and the general.

It was only midmorning when Jeff switched off his camera. "Gee, that was flawless. It's a shame this segment couldn't have been longer. You both just seemed to be getting wound up."

"I'm willing to go on if you are, Andy," the general surprised her by saying.

"I don't want you to strain yourself."

"Dad, you'd better stop before you get too tired."

"I'm fine, Lyon. Truly," the old man said, turning slightly in his chair to speak to his son, who was standing sentinel across the room. "Let's go on."

"Jeff?" Andy asked.

"I'm ready. I love this setting."

They did another session and were finished before lunch.

Lyon had seen his father to his bedroom, where they were going to eat their lunch off a tray. Gracie served Andy and the crew in the dining room. They were sitting over glasses of iced tea, discussing the next day's schedule and the tapes that were already done.

"He's sharper than I expected," Jeff said, spitting out an olive pit. "When Les told me the old guy was ninety, I thought, Jeez, what are we going to do with him if he nods off or something?"

Andy bristled. "He's anything but senile, Jeff."

"Don't get all hot and bothered, Andy. I didn't mean anything."

"His sense of humor's something I didn't expect. Like yesterday when he admitted he wasn't a very good shot," Gil said diplomatically.

"It's hotter than hell down here," Tony grumbled. His complaint was ignored.

"I just wonder what the old man's hiding," Jeff said offhandedly.

The words could have been a bomb, judging by the impact they had on Andy. "What do you mean?" she said, turning to him with a swift jerking motion. "Why would you think he's hiding something?"

Jeff shrugged. "Les said he wouldn't talk about the war, that he might have some secret that he didn't want anyone to know about."

"Les is crazy. You know he gets these wild notions."

"That usually turn out to be right," Jeff said.

"Not this time."

"Are you sure? Les said you were going to get chummy with the son to see if you could eke any info out of him. How 'bout it? Find out any juicy tidbits?"

A sound from behind them brought their attention around. Lyon was standing in the archway leading into the hall. His eyes were almost black as he glared at Andy. He was clutching his straw hat with both hands. Ten knuckles were white.

"I wanted to offer you the use of the pool this afternoon," he said. The brittle words seemed to have a hard time finding their way out of the taut lips. "There are suits, towels, anything you need in the cabana." He put the hat on and pulled it down low over his brows, thankfully screening his accusing eyes from Andy. His boot heels echoed like the strokes of a death knell on the tile as he went out the front door.

Tony whistled softly through his teeth.

Gil shifted uncomfortably and looked at his empty plate.

Warren cleared his throat.

Jeff chuckled. "Well, well, well. I think we've riled the cowboy."

"Shut up, Jeff." Andy snapped.

"Touchy, touchy. What's with you two?"

Play it cool, Andy, and don't you dare cry in front of them. Don't think about the hatred you saw on Lyon's face. Don't think about the kisses you've exchanged with a man who now seems to hold you in contempt. Don't think!

"He seems friendly enough," Gil said, seeming not to notice that Andy hadn't answered Jeff's question. "But I get the feeling he'd just as soon we weren't here."

"He was dead-set against the whole idea at first, but as you see, he's come around." She took a sip of her tea with as much nonchalance as she could muster.

"Did you learn anything from him?"

"No. I didn't get chummy, either. Les is way off base this time."

"Is he?"

"Yes," she fairly screamed. For the second time in only a few hours, she pushed away from the dining table in a high state of agitation. "Why don't all of you go swimming? I'll join you in an hour or so, after I've read over my notes for tomorrow. Warren, is the monitor set up so that I can play the tapes back?"

"Yeah, Andy. In the living room."

"Thank you. See you all later."

Ostensibly in her room to review her notes, she brooded instead. Below her windows she could hear the laughter and playful splashing of the crew, but she was disinclined to join them in the pool.

Lyon had overheard Jeff. Now he'd never believe that their intimacy was anything more than a ploy to get him to talk about his father. He had never trusted her. What Jeff had said would only confirm in Lyon's mind that she was a schemer, a ruthless opportunist who didn't care whom she hurt so long as she got her story.

Lying on her bed, her arm across her eyes, she groaned when Gracie tapped on her door and said, "Andy, a Mr. Trapper is holding on the line for you. Do you want to talk to him?"

No. "Yes. Tell him I'll be right there. Can I take the call on the extension in the hall?"

"Sure. I'll hang up when I hear you."

"Thank you, Gracie." She hauled herself off the bed and tried to shake off the lethargy that threatened to anchor her to the mattress. In her stocking feet she padded into the hallway and picked up the receiver. "Hello, Les." She heard Gracie break her connection.

"Hello, baby doll. How is everything?"

"Fine."

"Crew get there without mishap?"

"Yes, they arrived very early yesterday morning." Too early. Why couldn't they have arrived an hour later? Then maybe Lyon. . . .

"How's the taping going?"

"Fine. We've got three in the can. The general's wonderful."

"No equipment trouble?"

"No. Yesterday Gil had a dead cord, but he drove down to San Antonio and got another one. Everything's fine now."

There was a sustained pause in the conversation while Les digested everything she'd said. She wondered where Lyon was, what he was doing.

"Andy baby, it makes me nervous as hell when every thing is going just 'fine.'"

"I don't know what you mean." She knew exactly what he meant. Usually she was bubbling with excitement over what she was doing, or boiling with anger over the uncooperative weather, or griping about a technical breakdown, or laughing over something that had happened to a crewman. But she was never apathetic.

"I like for little disasters to happen every now and then to keep everybody on their toes. Know what I mean? You sound like you could use a big dose of either Geritol or milk of magnesia or Midol. When things are so damn 'fine,' I get skittish. What in hell is going on down there?"

No more Mr. Nice Guy. His glasses had been flung to the top of his desk. His feet had hit the floor hard. One hand was plowing through his mop of red hair. His eyes were boring a hole into the door of his office, in lieu of her hide. Ordinarily she would be sitting in the chair opposite his desk. Being a thousand miles away from Les's wrath had distinct advantages.

"Les, calm down. Nothing is going on except the interviews, which are going very well. The crew feels as I do about the general and were surprised by his astuteness. If anything is bothering me personally, it's the heat. It's energy-draining."

"What about Hopalong Lyon?"

Her palms were sweaty. "What about him?"

"Find out anything from him?"

She sighed in exasperation, hoping that if she sounded annoyed, he wouldn't hear the tremor in her voice. "Les, for the hundredth time, there's nothing to find out."

"I saw his picture."

"Whose?"

"Lyon Ratliff's. A picture of him in Nam that the AP supplied. He's a hunk."

"I haven't really noticed."

"If I was a woman, I'd have noticed."

"Well as you remind us far too often, you're an extremely virile man, so your opinion on the subject doesn't count. Now, Les, if there's nothing more, the crew is calling me to join them in the pool." They weren't, but it sounded more like her old self to say so.

"They're not down there for a vacation. Don't they have anything better to do?"

"Not after we're through for the day."

"Okay," he grumbled "Andy, you wouldn't keep anything important from your ol' buddy Les, now would you?"

Instantly on her guard, she laughed, searching through her blank mind for something clever to say. "Of course not. I think you're disappointed and jealous that we're all having such a good time down here." She laughed again, but she was the only one laughing, and it sounded hollow and insincere. "I'll call you back tomorrow and report in. Okay?"

"Okay. Bye, baby. Love ya."

The phone went dead in her hand.

Knowing it would be just like Les to call one of the crew to check up on her and verify everything she'd told him, she knew that sulking in her room was a bad idea. Much as she wanted to avoid company, she put on a strapless terry-cloth jumpsuit and went to the poolside. She sat in the shade of an umbrella over a wrought-iron table. Periodically she smoothed tanning lotion on spots that couldn't be reached, fetched towels, and offered unsolicited coaching on diving technique.

Late in the afternoon, Gracie brought out a pitcher of frozen margaritas and a platter of nachos. Jeff, dripping water, hugged her to him and kissed her on the cheek.

Andy had never seen him blush, but he did so profusely when he turned away from Gracie and she swatted him on the behind with a resounding whack.

Lyon drove up in his battered Jeep. He rolled out of it with lithe grace and sauntered over to the pool. "How's the water?"

"Great," Jeff called. "Join us."

"Sorry. I've got a date."

Andy kept her eyes glued to the book she had brought down with her, but the words blurred in front of her eyes. Her heart plummeted to her stomach and lay there like a stone.

"Gracie told me she's serving you Mexican food out here on the patio. Enjoy it. I'll see you in the morning."

Everyone called their good-byes, including Andy. Intending to show him she didn't care if or with whom he had a date, she glanced up at him through the large lenses of her sunglasses. Though the brim of his hat cast his face in deep shadow, she knew his eyes were riveted on her. "Have fun," she called brightly, as much for the benefit of her crew as for Lyon.

"I will," he said firmly, grinning at her sardonically and leaving no doubt in her mind what kind of fun he'd be pursuing. Then he turned his back on her.

The pain in her chest was so severe, she didn't start breathing again until long after she'd heard his footsteps disappear into the house.

Gracie's enchiladas, tacos, and guacamole were delicious, but Andy didn't taste anything. Soon after the food

135

had been demolished, the crew bade her good night and headed toward the bunkhouse, where a rousing poker game was scheduled. She wandered through the house after Gracie refused her offer to help in the kitchen. The general had been in bed for hours. She tried not to think about Lyon and who he was with and what they were doing.

Did he go out regularly? Someone specific? Had he called someone today and made the date for tonight? Would women be willing to go out with him on that short notice? Yes. She would have been. Why hadn't he asked her out?

The answer to that was painfully simple. All too clearly, he'd demonstrated his dislike. The tenderness with which he'd kissed her that morning in her bedroom had been the result of a mood that would never be recaptured. Once he'd remembered who she was and what she was doing in his house, he'd been filled with self-disgust and bitterness. If he chose to believe her manipulative and grasping, then there was nothing she could do at this point to prove him wrong. Strangely she lacked the energy to try.

At eleven o'clock, after filling the long, lonely hours with daydreams of what could never be, she despairingly climbed the stairs to her room.

And at twelve o'clock she was still wide awake, and she decided to avail herself of the pool after all, hoping that a few brisk laps would exhaust her enough to sleep.

Wearing her discreet bikini, which was nonetheless provocative on her lush figure, she went down the stairs, out the back door, and into the pool. All was dark, and she didn't turn on any lights.

The water caressed her ankles, calves, and thighs. Then she did a surface dive and swam the length of the pool underwater. Coming up for air, she kicked away from the side and swam with even strokes, back and forth three times. She brought herself to the surface, leading with her chin to pull her hair out slick behind her. Leaning her head against the mosaic tiles just above the waterline, she drew in deep breaths.

Only then did she see Lyon, and her heart, which was already pounding with exertion, accelerated even faster. He was standing at the opposite end of the pool. The sport coat that was hooked over his shoulder by an index finger was tossed into a lounge chair. The necktie was whipped from beneath his shirt collar and he began unbuttoning his shirt.

"What are you doing?" she asked on a high, breathless note.

Chapter Seven

❧

What does it look like I'm doing?" The unbuttoned shirt was pulled out of the waistband of his slacks. He worked his feet out
of a pair of dress loafers and raised each
foot in turn to peel off his socks. Next came the lizard
belt; it was whisked through the belt loops and joined the
growing heap on the lounge chair. Never for an instant
did his eyes leave hers. Even through the darkness she
felt their impaling power.

His fingers loosed his trousers with dispatch, and he proceeded to step out of them. Andy, watching his act with
stunned disbelief, heard her own breathing as rapid panting.

He folded the trousers and laid them on the back of the
chair. His thumbs hooked into either side of his underwear.

"I'm not going to scream, you know," she said haughtily. She knew that this entire scene had been planned and executed to unnerve her. "I've seen a naked man before."

Unswayed, he said silkily, "You've seen me naked before. And I think you liked it. I think you'd like a second look." The underwear was discarded.

What he'd suggested was true. The second look was better than the first. His broad shoulders narrowed only slightly in the chest, then his long lean trunk tapered to slender hips. His legs, dusted with the same dark hair that covered his chest, were straight and hard, each muscle and tendon honed to perfection by constant, strenuous use.

He did a foolhardy dive off the shallow end and torpedoed under the water the length of the pool until he slowly surfaced inches from her. His hair clung to his head like a snug, dark cap.

He was so dangerously, sexily magnetic that Andy felt compelled to retreat. She bent her knee with the intention of pushing away from the wall and going around him. His arms came up on either side of her, pinning her between the side of the pool and his equally unyielding flesh.

"No, no, Ms. Malone. We're going to have a little chat."

"You're home early. Didn't your date invite you in for a cup of coffee?" she asked nastily.

"As a matter of fact she did."

"I'll bet."

"But I turned down the refill."

"A pity."

"Not exactly," he drawled. His legs drifted closer to hers. She felt the hairs, like harbingers of caresses yet to come, tickle her skin only a moment before his thighs were rubbing against hers. "I figured why go to all that bother when there's someone under my own roof ready to do anything for the sake of research?"

His words were spoken softly, but his eyes glittered like slate. Rarely had Andy Malone been afraid. Her self-confidence didn't leave much room for a weak emotion like that. Cautious, yes. Fearful, no. Now, with Lyon's hard body radiating anger like a furnace, she was afraid.

"You're wrong. I'm not ready to do anything with you."

He laughed without humor. "Oh, yes, you are." His eyes dropped to her breasts, swelling voluptuously over the top of the bikini. "You've been waving the red flag at the bull for days. It's time you came across." Before she could stop him, he had thrust his hand beneath the fabric and lifted her breast loose from the material.

"Lyon, no," she cried softly.

"Yes." His mouth came down on hers hard, savagely, angrily. His tongue was like a whip, lashing and stinging her mouth everywhere it struck. She tried to twist free, but his hand tangling in her wet hair forbade it. His mouth persisted with that punishing, bruising kiss while the hand on her breast insulted her. Unlike this morning in her room, when his touch had been almost worshipful, he fondled her now with careless disdain.

His body closed what small space remained between them, and cemented her to the side of the pool. He forced her thighs apart. From chest to knees he pressed her to him lustfully.

"You're going to have to do better than this, Ms. Malone. You want to know all my deep, dark secrets, don't you? Aren't they worth more to you than one uncooperative kiss? Hm?"

The violation began again. The kiss was harder. He released her hair to slide his hand down her back to her hips, which he molded to his palm as he fastened her body to his. She felt the flat, hair-silky plane of his stomach muscles against her own. His heaving breaths matched her own. And against her middle—oh, God— a hard and insistent pressure that declared him man and her woman.

Despite the violence of the embrace, despite his anger and her wounded spirit, she felt desire beginning to un- coil and snake through her body. She fought it, cursed herself, cursed him for awakening such a treacherous frailty. Yet even as her mind hardened against him, her body softened and became malleable.

He lifted his head immediately when she ceased to struggle. Long, ponderous moments ticked by as he watched her, asking a million silent questions that she an- swered with sincerity pouring like tears out of her golden eyes, past the wet, spiky lashes. He placed his hands on the deck of the pool and floated the length of his arms away from her, allowing her to escape him if she chose.

She didn't. All her attention was focused on him. Slowly he inclined his head toward her. Touching only her mouth, he kissed her. Gone was the brutality. He conquered this time, not with force, but with finesse, his tongue an instrument of pleasure that ignited deeply embedded fires as it caressed the inside of her mouth in symbolic penetration.

Her hands came up like a blind man's to touch the rigid planes of his face, hoping to find the mellow expression that she had seen before. Momentarily he closed his eyes and allowed her fingertips to wander as they would, exploring, examining . . . loving.

She traced the arch of the sleek black brows, the bridge of the nose, the sensual curve of his mouth. His lips opened and caught a daring fingertip between them. He worried the pad of it with his teeth, then with his tongue. She held her breath as his tongue stroked downward the entire length of her finger and then slid between the base of it and the next one, stroking the sensitive skin. She uttered a small cry, and her body reflexively arched against his. His eyes flew open.

Then he was kissing her again, with hunger tamed by tenderness. His hand found her breasts again, bared now by his swift and careful removal of the bikini top. Her nipples became firm and erect in his palms as he covered her. His caressing fingers rewarded them for their ready response. Gently, gently.

She made no protest when his hand slid beneath the bottom of her bikini and eased it down over her hips. With slow, graceful movements of her legs between his, it floated free. He clasped her nakedness to his. Desire was kept banked for a moment as they delighted only in the feel of each other, contrasting textures, forms.

He released her to hoist himself over the edge of the pool, then extended his hand and helped lift her out of the water. Dripping, he led them into the darkened cabana. They didn't speak, lest they alert anyone to this midnight tryst. Not that either of them at that moment was ashamed of what was about to happen, only that it was too precious, too private, to share.

He squeezed her hand and then released it. In the darkness he found the large bath sheets stored in the closet. Taking one out, he quickly spread it on the wide lounge in the cool, dark room. She approached him in the dark. He sat on the lounge, took her hand again, and pulled her toward him.

Moonlight was her only garment as he caressed her. The fullness of her breasts, their aroused crests, were admired and adored. His hands encircled her rib cage, and he massaged his thumbs down the furrow between them.

"Appendectomy?" he asked, tracing the thin scar on her abdomen.

"Yes."

Turning her around, his teeth took a delicate bite out of the side of her waist. Pivoting her again, he kissed her where her spine curved into the small of her back. His mouth opened over the skin lightly sprinkled with white down. He dragged his tongue through it.

"Lyon," she breathed.

He brought her back around to face him and leaned forward, his mouth hovering over her navel. He delved into it with his tongue and found a few drops of water there.

He looked up at her and smiled. "Chlorine never tasted so good."

She laughed softly and riffled through his hair, which was drying now. Her laughter became short, halting breaths as his kisses continued across her belly to her thighs. This lack of restraint was new to her. Robert had seen her naked, of course, but she never remembered a time when she had stood like this and watched as he adored her nudity. Never had his hands caressed, nor his lips kissed the way Lyon's were. Nor would she have welcomed such intimacy.

Why then was she standing in tingling excitement and allowing him to do this? Why was her heart expanding with pride in her body, when she'd always been self-conscious about her femininity before? When he lay down and urged her to join him, she didn't resist, but settled naturally along his length.

"I was watching you swim," he said as he idly stroked her spine with his fingertips.

"I didn't see you." Her palms flattened over the sculptured chest and rotated slowly.

"You weren't supposed to." Her lobe was captured by nipping teeth and then laved by a capricious tongue. "I sat perfectly still when I saw you come out." He groaned when her fingernail skated across one flat, brown nipple.

145

"Among other things," he grated as she kept up that bliss-ful torment, "you swim very well."

"Thank you."

He kissed her as his hand appreciated the line of her thigh. His mouth was hot and urgent, his tongue probing. Her lips closed around it and sucked gently. He groaned again. "God, Andy." He lifted his mouth only far enough to tease the corner of her lips with nibbling kisses.

Much as she didn't want to destroy the kindling desire, she wanted to break down any barriers between them, eliminate any misunderstanding. "Lyon . . . oh . . . what are you doing? Are you . . . touching . . ."

"You feel so good," he murmured against her throat.

His gentle manipulations were educating her to a level of sensuality she'd never known before. Throwing inhi-bitions aside, she moved against his hand. "Lyon, please . . . wait. I want to explain . . . ah, Lyon."

"Later, Andy. It can wait." His lips moved against her nipple before he flicked it with his tongue. Then stroking it to the beat of the erotic rhythm of his fingertips at the portal of her womanhood, he robbed her of logical thought, and her senses took command of her brain. "That's it. Give it all over to feeling," he whispered in her ear as he lifted himself over her.

Instinct directed her, though she loved Lyon's gentle commands. Robert had been a quick, silent lover. She knew a momentary panic that she might disappoint Lyon as she had Robert. What she had discussed during inter-views with experts on human sexuality, she'd never been able to relate to herself. She'd certainly never tried a practical application of anything she'd discussed so openly and candidly. Perhaps she wasn't a whole woman. Perhaps she couldn't . . .

But as Lyon's body sank into hers, and she felt his shudder of gratification, her worries were obliterated by the thrill of having him inside her.

"Andy," he moaned, "you're so right." While his body remained completely motionless he raised his head from her shoulder to look at her. His eyes traveled over her face in the way they had often done. Propping himself up on one arm, his hand moved between their bodies and found her breast. "You take me so well," he said softly.

Her throat arched and her head went back as he played with the distended bud that swelled even more between his fingers. He dipped his head to reward it. Her response rippled through her body, and he began to move. He touched her in a way she'd never been touched before. Not only physically, but spiritually, and she gave herself up to it.

She knew. In spite of their inauspicious meeting, his mistrust, his sarcasm, his rankling taunts, and the anger they had engendered in her, she loved this man. If she had not, she would have been able to ignore the insults he had heaped on her. She would have disregarded his threats that she tread lightly in her interviews with his father. But because she loved him, his insults had been like mortal wounds to her. His threats had been useless, because she would have done nothing to hurt him. It would have been like hurting herself.

She wouldn't be with him now, engaged in this sacred rite of loving, if it were not for love. Les had often asked her who she was saving herself for. Now she knew. It wasn't for want of opportunity that she hadn't been involved with a man since Robert's death. It was for want of loving. She loved Lyon Ratliff.

Having defined this emotion, which ran so high each time she saw him and that brought pain each time they hurt each other, she met each thrust of his body lovingly.

"Yes, yes, darling." His breath was a rattling breeze in her ear. Her arms hugged him tighter, her thighs closed against his. "Andy, Andy, yes . . . yes. Lift . . . Oh, God, yes. So good."

A wellspring was building up inside her, roiling and bubbling like those that fed the river. This fountain was unknown to her. She'd never encountered it before and was shy of it. It threatened to drown her, but she couldn't fight its rushing current. It engulfed her heart, her throat, her mind, and just before it inundated her, she heard Lyon cry her name. She clutched at him tightly, and they were plunged beneath the surface together.

Long minutes later, lying still interlocked, breathing deeply of the same air in unison, he said again, "Andy . . .?"

And this time she was able to answer. "Yes, Lyon. Yes."

"Satisfied?"

"Yes," she said primly, taking the retrieved bikini out of his hand. The top had been found right away near the filter of the pool. The bottom had been elusive, requiring Lyon to make several searching dives. "I'll sleep much better now."

"Don't bet on it," he growled, grabbing her from behind and pulling her against his chest.

"Don't bet on what?" she asked provocatively, running her fingers up his ribs.

"Don't bet on sleeping." He kissed her soundly, then pushed her away. "Get inside. You're going to freeze." They had wrapped in extra large towels from the cabana and were now sneaking through the dark house and up the staircase. Lyon carried his clothes in one arm and draped the other across her bare shoulders.

She hesitated at the door to her bedroom, but he ushered her farther down the hall to his room. He closed the door behind them, crossed over to the bed, and turned on a bedside lamp.

"At last. Now I can see you in the light."

He padded over to her and reached for the towel she had tucked between her breasts. She stayed his hands by clasping his wrists. "Lyon, wait. Please."

Now that she knew she loved him, it bothered her more than ever to think he might not trust her. She couldn't bear it if he thought the motive for her surrender was anything but love. Any other reason would be so ludicrous, she couldn't believe he'd think that, not after the fierceness of their lovemaking in the cabana only half an hour ago. But she had to make sure.

"Why?" he asked softly.

"Because I want to talk to you." The immediate suspicious lowering of his brows confirmed her anxiety that she might still be suspect. Taking his hand, she led him to the bed and sat down. She sat with her knees together, her head bowed, looking down at her hands as she pleated the hem of the towel between her fingers. "You're mistaken."

"About what?" He sat at the end of the bed, his back braced against the bedpost.

"About what you think of me. I know you heard Jeff this afternoon."

"You mean the part about getting chummy with me in order to pump me for information?"

"Yes. That's not the case."

"Les didn't ask you to do that?"

She swallowed and looked at him, then quickly away. "Yes. He did. But I don't always listen to him. Not even as frequently as before," she added almost to herself.

Now she looked straight at Lyon, turning slightly to face him. "I've never had to prostitute myself for a story. In the first place I have a higher regard for myself than that. I was brought up to respect my body. I never considered it as something to barter with.

"But even disregarding the morality of it, I've never had to resort to so desperate a measure. I'm a professional. Some have been reluctant to bare their souls in front of a camera, but usually I've been able to persuade them to do so without coercion of any kind.

"I'm good at my work. I'm ambitious, though now . . . never mind. Anyway I like getting a story or an incisive interview that no one else has been able to get, but I don't have the ruthlessness, the go-for-the-jugular instinct that Les does. It's corny, but I've always advocated the saying about vinegar and honey. To my knowledge I've never seriously harmed anyone with one of my interviews, nor have I ever abused the privilege of confidentiality."

She sat still and waited. Before her monologue was finished, he had stood up and begun pacing at the foot of the bed. Now he stopped and sat down again. "You have to admit that the evidence is pretty incriminating. Not long after your conversation with Les, you warmed up to me considerably."

"I know. That had nothing to do with Les. The only time I've even thought of Les when I was with you was when you asked me who he was. Up to that point he was the furthest thing from my mind." She looked at him earnestly. "Lyon, do you really think I would try to exploit what happened a while ago? Do you think it meant no more to me than that?"

She felt tears shimmering in her eyes. "I know you're wary of women after what Jerri did, but don't condemn me unfairly. I pulled a childish stunt to get into this house. I'll admit that. But I haven't been playing games with you."

He watched one tear as it lost its precarious grip on her lower lid and began to roll down her cheek. He lifted it off with his fingertip and then brought it to his lips and sucked it into his mouth. "Will you take off that towel now?"

She cried out in relief and, still vacillating between laughter and tears, fell against him. They managed to get rid of the towels, pull down the bedspread and blankets, and slide between the sheets without breaking the kiss.

His strong arms encompassed her. The quickening pulse and shortness of breath that were now becoming familiar seized her again. She and Lyon fell on each other like starving beasts of prey. He rolled them both over to one side of the bed, then to the other, their mouths and bodies glued together.

When at last they drew apart, he was content to lie docilely and let her be the aggressor. Her mouth impressed fervent kisses into his throat. Seductively she lowered herself along his body until she reached his chest. Moving her head from side to side, she let the warm chest hair caress her features. She kissed his breastbone. Lifting her head slightly, she studied his nipple as her finger touched it. Then she followed suit with her tongue, delicately at first before a newfound courage dictated that she apply more pressure.

"Andy," he rasped and closed his arms around her, pulling her on top of him. He scorched a trail of avid kisses along the top curve of her breasts, working his way up to her mouth. "You're creating a monster, Andy Malone," he said into her mouth as his lips teasingly avoided hers. "A sex-crazed monster."

"What do sex-crazed monsters do?" She leaned forward to provide him access to her straining nipples.

"Ravish gorgeous women." His hands smoothed over her hips to curve around the backs of her thighs.

"Am I gorgeous?"

"Yes."

"Well, then?"

They slept for a while, the deep, dreamless sleep of satisfaction. He nudged her awake only a few hours later when an arc of sunlight spread across the wide bed.

"You'd better go to your room. We need to keep up the pretense of propriety."

"I don't want to," she said, snuggling against him and pressing her breasts against his side.

He moaned. "Andy stop that, dammit."

She giggled and struggled to separate her tangled limbs from his. "You old fuddy-duddy."

She sprang out of bed, but not before he slapped her on the fanny. "I'll see you downstairs for breakfast, won't I?" she asked, wrapping up in the towel and getting her bikini.

"If I can still walk."

She winked at him wickedly and swayed with a saucy gait to the door. She blew him a kiss before checking the hallway and then hurrying down it to her room.

She took special care with her toilette, bathing in scented water and styling her freshly washed hair in a more casual style. She'd dress for the interviews later. For breakfast she put on a bright cotton print sundress. She felt totally feminine today and wanted to proclaim to the world her womanhood, which had only blossomed to full bloom under Lyon's tender nurturing.

She was humming a catchy tune when she skipped out into the hallway and collided with a waiting Lyon. His arm surrounded her waist, and his mouth swooped down for a possessive kiss that stole her breath away.

"On your way to breakfast?" she asked when he at last released her.

"I could be persuaded to skip it."

"I couldn't. I'm starving."

They nuzzled and their hips bumped together as they wrapped their arms around each other's waists and started down the stairs. Halfway down they saw that Gracie was conversing with someone at the door. Andy's animation died. Her light footsteps became leaden. Panic stopped her heart and clogged her throat.

She couldn't see the man. Gracie's generous figure was blocking him from her view. But she could see the top of his head. Only one person had hair that shade of red.

Les Trapper.

Chapter Eight

❦

She stumbled against Lyon and gripped the bannister. Should Les find out about her and Lyon, his suspicions would increase a hundredfold. He would jump to the conclusion that her objectivity had been compromised. It hadn't been, but there would be no convincing Les of that.

He had no jurisdiction over her life. She was free to love whoever she wanted, but her being with Lyon last night had put her credibility in jeopardy. She'd have to play the consummate professional and put Les off the track. There was no time to explain that to Lyon now. Surely he would understand.

Before she could talk herself out of it, she shoved away from him and took the last few steps on a run. "Les!" she cried.

He spied her over Gracie's broad shoulder and side-stepped the housekeeper to meet Andy halfway. She flew into his warm embrace. He kissed her roundly on the mouth. *Would he taste Lyon there?* she thought in panic.

"Andy baby, Lord, but I've missed you, sweetheart," he exclaimed, hugging her tighter.

"I've missed you, too." She had been lying so often lately. Hopefully without arousing his suspicions, she eased out of his arms. "What are you doing here? And this early in the morning?"

"I got a red-eye flight out of Nashville and made it to San Antonio last night. I drove the rest of the way this morning."

"I guess everyone's going to want coffee." Gracie had never sounded so ungracious. She was glaring at Les with undisguised resentment.

"Please, Gracie." The deep voice came from above them on the stairs.

Les's red head went up and back as he noticed Lyon for the first time. Andy's heart swelled with pride as she watched him descend the stairs with the ease and grace of a proud man. A man in a three-piece business suit couldn't look any more distinguished than Lyon did wearing his faded jeans and cotton shirt. The sleeves had been rolled up to the elbows to reveal the strong arms that had held her through the night. His dark hair shone in the sunlight that was filtering through the windows. It had been well brushed but was already getting out of control.

She heard Gracie huffing off to get the coffee, but Andy's attention didn't waver from the two men as they confronted each other. The way they measured each other could only be defined as a confrontation. Lyon was taller, leaner, brawnier, but Les exuded the cunning of a street fighter.

Their dislike for each other was instantaneous and intense, and the air practically crackled with it. So palpable was it that Andy had to clear her throat in the suddenly dense atmosphere before she said, "Ly . . . Mr. Ratliff, this is Les Trapper, my producer. Les, Lyon Ratliff."

Lyon stepped down to floor level, but didn't extend his hand. "Mr. Trapper," he said by way of greeting.

"Lyon." The casual use of Lyon's first name was intended as an affront, and Lyon took it as such. Andy could see that he was bristling, even though he was clearly trying to conceal his reactions from them both. "Thank you for taking care of Andy for me," Les said, placing a protective, possessive arm across her shoulders.

Lyon's steely eyes stabbed into her and she wanted to cry out in protest at the accusation in them. *No, no, Lyon, none of this has anything to do with last night.*

"Ms. Malone impresses me as a woman who can take care of herself."

"That she can," Les said heartily. "After all, she convinced you and your father to grant her an interview that others have tried to get and failed. Speaking of which, I have some good news. One of the networks got wind of the project and has offered to buy the whole kit and caboodle from the cable company."

Andy turned to him in surprise. "Are you kidding?"

"No," Les laughed. His blue eyes were sparkling behind the lenses of his glasses. "They want to see the interviews before they make a firm offer, but they're *very* interested. The management of the cable company is willing to sell them if they get credit for them."

Andy wondered why she wasn't dancing with jubilation. This was her dream come true. This is what she had worked for, hoped for, for years. Why was she only moderately happy? Les was looking at her quizzically. *Play the part, Andy.* She threw her arms around his neck and hugged him tight. "Les, that is wonderful!" she exclaimed and hoped that her words didn't ring as hollow in his ears as they did in hers.

"If you'll excuse me," Lyon said with all the repugnance and scorn in the world wrapped around his exit line. He stalked through the door that led into the kitchen. Andy knew Les was still watching her carefully, so she refrained from looking after him mournfully. Every impulse in her body was urging her to run to him. *Later, when this is over with, I'll make him understand.*

Les snapped his fingers in front of her nose. "Hey, remember me?"

She looked up with a smile that she thought might very well crack her face. "Ready for coffee?" she said brightly, turning toward the same door Lyon had used.

"Not so fast," Les said, grabbing her arm and turning her around. "What's going on here?"

"W—what do you mean?" She hoped her perplexed expression looked more genuine than it felt.

"I mean that something here isn't right, and I want to know what it is."

"Les, you're shooting in the dark," she said trying to pass off her alarm as impatience. Les mustn't find out, mustn't guess. "What could be wrong?"

"I don't know," he said slowly, eyeing her with clinical bemusement. "But I intend to find out. Like why did you look like you'd seen a ghost when you came barrelling down the stairs? That in itself was unlike you. I'm thrilled that you're glad to see me, but something—"

"Les, really, you're going daft. Ever since I came down here, you've been talking like Ellery Queen, searching for clues to something that doesn't exist."

"Yeah, helluva coincidence, isn't it? That *I* started acting like a whacko the minute *you* got to Texas."

She was saved from making a reply when Jeff pushed through the kitchen door. "Hey, Les! Gracie said you were here. It's a real occasion when you pry yourself away from that garbage heap you call a desk."

Les expounded on the whys and wherefores of his unexpected appearance, which Andy knew to be contrived. He was there for one reason and one reason only. To check up on her.

She was relieved that Lyon had excused himself from having breakfast with them. He had already left for his day's work on the ranch by the time she, Les, and Jeff filed into the dining room to join the rest of the crew. Over Gracie's delicious breakfast they discussed the taping session planned for that day.

"We should be able to finish up by tomorrow afternoon," Andy said. "We'll do the interview by the river tomorrow morning. That will be the last one. Jeff, have you got enough B roll?"

Les made suggestions and asked to watch the tapes already "in the can." As they were draining their last cups of coffee General Ratliff wheeled into the dining room. He had taken his meal in his room. As always he was impeccably groomed, but Andy didn't like his color. His complexion had a waxy sheen that concerned her.

She introduced him to Les, who responded politely and quietly. She left them to get acquainted while the crew went about setting up their equipment in the living room and she went upstairs to dress and apply her makeup.

Half an hour later they were ready to begin. She was well into her introductory remarks when Les interrupted. "Wait a minute, wait a minute," he said. Jeff cursed and raised his head from the viewfinder of his camera. "General, excuse me but you don't look like a military man," Les said. "Don't you have a uniform or anything?"

"We've already discussed that with the general, Les," Andy said smoothly. "He prefers not to wear one."

"Why?" Bluntness was one of Les's virtues—or vices.

"Because, for one thing, they're forty years old and he hasn't had them on since he retired."

"Then couldn't he just hold one, or have one hanging behind him or something?"

"General?" Andy asked softly. "Would you object to that?"

"I suppose not," he said. He gave her a tired smile and patted her hand. "If you want to hang a uniform behind me, that will be fine."

"Great!" Les said, clapping his hands together. "Where's Gracie?"

"I'll get a uniform." Andy was relieved that Lyon wasn't in the room when they started. She didn't realize that he had come in until he spoke. She watched as he stamped from the room to find the uniform that she damned Les for mentioning.

Gil took advantage of the break to adjust the general's microphone higher on his lapel. His voice wasn't as strong today as it had been. Gil was just stepping back when Lyon came in carrying a general's uniform that smelled faintly of mothballs, but was pressed and in mint condition.

She caught Lyon's eye as he hung it behind them where Les directed him. Silently she pleaded for him to understand the reason for everything that she had done from the time she had left his arms to run to Les. But looking into his eyes was like looking into mirrors. She could see only a distressed reflection of herself and not into the soul of the man she loved.

Had she told him she loved him? During all those passionate hours of the night before had she spoken of love?

161

Maybe if she had told him what was in her heart, he wouldn't be looking at her with such hatred now.

He jerked his head in Les's direction. "Get him to lay off Dad. Understand, Ms. Malone?" he sneered. Then he was backing away and Les was saying how much better the set looked with the uniform establishing the mood, and somehow she got through the interview.

As soon as it was done, she went up to her room to change back into the sundress. The linen suit she had worn for the interview had started to feel cloying and restricting. Yet after changing, she realized that the tightening pressure was on the inside, not out. She felt that all her organs were clamped between the jaws of a great beast and that the life was slowly being squeezed out of them.

She stood at the window and gazed out at the beautiful landscape. She didn't feel any kinship with the woman who had come to this house a few days earlier and stood at this window for the first time. She no longer existed.

In her place was Andy Malone, a woman who had been born only a few hours ago. She didn't want her old life back. A life of loneliness, empty motel rooms, solitary meals. Her dream of being in the limelight of network programming paled against the glowing warmth of Lyon's love. Ambition seemed no longer an asset, but a burden she longed to cast aside.

"Penny for them." Les came into the room unannounced, crossed to the window, took her hand, and led her to the bed. She sat down on the edge of it and listlessly let him massage her neck with his large hands. "Worth more than a penny?"

"Much more."

"Must be good."

"No, not so good."

"Wanna tell me about it?"

"Maybe sometime. Not now."

"It breaks my heart, you know."

She turned her head and looked up at him, not able to picture Les with a broken heart over anything. "What breaks your heart?"

"That you don't confide in me anymore. Hell, Andy, I thought we were a team. After all we've been through together. Robert's death. Everything." He was rubbing her neck hypnotically, and she dropped her chin against her chest and closed her eyes. "Is it Robert? Do you still miss him?"

She shook her head. "No, nothing like that, Les." She asked something she'd never been able to bring herself to ask before. "Did you know he ran around on me?"

For a long minute the hands around her neck were still, then began their stroking again. "Yeah. I didn't know you knew. That was the only thing Robert and I ever fought about. I raised hell with him when I found out about it."

"You shouldn't have blamed him. It wasn't all his fault. It"—she swallowed—"it never was very good."

"Maybe he was the wrong guy." The hands were still once again.

She lifted her head and looked up at him. His blue eyes asked the pertinent question, and she shook her head.

"No, Les."

He shrugged and continued tracking his thumbs down the vertebrae at the base of her neck. "It was worth a try. I've always had a lech for you, you know. But you may look ugly as sin in bed."

She laughed. "Thanks, friend."

"'Course *you* wouldn't be disappointed. Not if we started with a Jell-O bath."

She chuckled again, glad that things were on a more even footing. This was familiar, this bantering. She could handle this now and deal with the heartache and splendor.

Lyon later. "A Jell-O bath?"

"Don't tell me you've never had one!" His hands closed on her shoulders, and he leaned down to tickle her neck with his nose. "I'll tell you all about it."

"I thought you probably would," she said drily.

"Everybody gets naked, see? Then you fill up the bathtub with gallons of squishy Jell-O." She was laughing in earnest now, both at his words and his gnawing lips on her neck. "I like green personally, because with red hair it's my best color, but some prefer—"

His words broke off abruptly, and his hands tensed. Andy's laughter died away, and she opened her eyes to look up at him. She followed the direction of his stare toward the doorway, where Lyon towered like a menacing giant.

Every muscle of his body was tensed, and he was rocking back and forth slightly, like an animal tethered on a chain that might give way any moment. His hands, bracing him between the jamb, looked as though they were ready to tear the wood away from the walls.

"Pardon the interruption," he said tersely. "Gracie asked that I round everyone up for lunch. I'll get the others." Then he was gone, and Andy was bleakly staring at the empty doorway.

Les bounded around the foot of the bed and with his index finger jerked her chin up until he was looking her fully in the face. "So that's the way the wind blows," he said. "He's got the hots for our little Andy, and she goes all marshmallowy every time he looks at her."

"No!"

"Oh, yes, Andrea Malone. Don't lie to me. I've got eyes, dammit, and I know jealousy when I see it. I was so sure that he was about to murder me, my life passed before my eyes." He began pacing in what everyone referred to as Les's "thinking" routine. "I should have known it was something like this. Those tapes I looked at this morning were good, but they're Mickey Mouse."

"There's nothing wrong with those interviews," she said heatedly.

"There's nothing terrific about them either," he shouted back. "You could be interviewing Bozo the Clown for all the information we have on his military career. You've gone soft, Andy, lost your objectivity, and it's because you want to shack up with Lyon."

There was small compensation in the fact that he didn't know she'd already been with Lyon. "I don't know how you can possibly imagine that. We've been butting heads since I first got near him. He has nothing but contempt for me."

"Then prove me wrong. Tomorrow morning, I want you to hit the old guy with all you've got. Hell, Andy, you could pry information out of a turnip and it wouldn't even know it had been had. I've seen you do it hundreds of times."

"The General's sick, Les—"

"And he has something to hide. I feel it in my gut. What was all that stink over wearing a uniform? Huh? It's not normal, and when something's not normal, I practically break out in a rash."

"I won't badger him," she said, shaking her head adamantly.

Les gripped her painfully by the shoulders. "Then I will, Andy. Getting General Michael Ratliff to reveal why he retired early and has lived in seclusion all these years could be our ticket to the network. You come across with the story of the year, or I will."

From downstairs they heard the others trooping through the hall to the dining room. Les released her with his hands, but not with his eyes. She felt them on her as they went downstairs and took their seats at the table. Lyon was seated at one end, but the general apparently was going to eat in his room.

Gracie hustled to get the food on the table and the crew fell to with appreciation. Andy pushed a forkful into her mouth, though her body was repelled by the idea of eating.

"Your father took an early retirement, didn't he, Lyon?" Les asked between bites of cold chicken salad.

Lyon finished chewing and swallowed. "Yes."

"Any particular reason?"

Andy shot Les a threatening look, but he didn't see it. He and Lyon were staring each other down like boxers assessing each other across the canvas.

"Ms. Malone asked him that," Lyon answered levelly. "He said he wanted to try another way of life, that he was tired of the military. He wanted to live at a less hectic pace, spend more time with my mother."

"But he was still young," Les argued.

The others around the table had grown quiet, listening to the conversation that vibrated with so many unspoken meanings. The crew had seen Les rake numerous intimidating people over the coals, but thought that perhaps this time he had bitten off more than he could chew. By anyone's estimation, Lyon Ratliff wasn't a man one would provoke unnecessarily.

"Perhaps that's why he got out when he did. He wanted to have plenty of time to ranch." Lyon took another bite of his lunch, dismissing the importance of Les's questions.

"Maybe," Les said in a tone that reeked of skepticism. Andy saw Lyon's hand tighten around his water glass. "On the other hand, it could have been for an entirely different reason. There could have been something he wasn't too keen on the rest of the world finding out. Maybe about your mother, or the war—"

Lyon's chair flew backward and fell to the floor with a crash. Silverware, crystal, and china clattered together on the table as his knee caught it from underneath. Andy heard Jeff's softly whispered, "Jeez." Gracie came running from the kitchen.

Lyon resembled a jealous god bent on vengeance. The heat of his fury surrounded him like an aura. His eyes flashed lightning. "I want you out of here by nightfall. Got it? Out." His eyes swung to Andy. "All of you. Do the last interview this afternoon, as soon as my father has rested, and then clear out." He stepped to the overturned chair and picked it up. "Sorry about the mess, Gracie." Then he stormed out of the room.

Silence prevailed even after Gracie tactfully withdrew into the kitchen.

Jeff cleared his throat. For once his cockiness was subdued. "We were planning on charging all our batteries tonight, Andy. I don't know if we'll have enough power to shoot—"

"Do the best you can, Jeff," she said vaguely.

"Okay. Sure." He stood up, and the others followed his lead. "We'll go on and set up where you showed us near river." They left.

She folded her napkin with perfect symmetry. It seemed very important that it be folded just right before she set it down beside her barely touched plate. She stood up.

"Andy—"

"Shut up, Les. I think you've said enough."

For the scene outside she had planned to wear something soft and more casual than the outfits she'd worn for the other scenes. She had asked the general not to put on his coat and tie, as well. More than any of the other sessions she had been looking forward to this one. The riverbank was such a lovely setting.

Now, it was to be the farewell interview, too, and that added a nostalgic quality to it. She'd never given a thought to the time she'd have to leave. She'd known that the time would come, but she'd never dwelled on it.

"Admit it, Andy," she said to herself in the mirror. "You hoped to go on seeing Lyon after you left."

Now she saw the fallacy in such wishful thinking. He had his life. She had hers. The directions in which they were going would never run parallel. Perhaps it was better that she leave with him thinking the worst of her. She didn't think she could have turned her back on him otherwise.

She dressed in toast-brown slacks and a yellow blouse. It was called a poet shirt because of its full, deeply cuffed sleeves, open throat, and blousy cut. She gathered her hair into a loose ponytail on the nape of her neck to add to the romantic look.

Everyone was waiting for her on the patio. General Ratliff was sitting in his wheelchair in the shade of the cabana. She diverted her eyes from the building. It brought back too many stirring memories. If she'd ever relied on professional detachment, she'd have to now. The tears were close to the surface. With the least amount of encouragement, she'd throw herself into Lyon's arms as he stood remote and stony, watching everything, saying nothing.

"I thought I'd get some B roll as the two of you walk down the path. The scenery is so pretty," Jeff said.

"That's fine," Andy said. "What do you want us to do?"

"Why don't you just walk alongside General Ratliff's chair and talk. I'll do the rest."

"All right."

The general had heard Jeff's directions and turned his chair onto the paved path. Andy fell into step beside him. She was going to mime the conversation, but the general surprised her by initiating it.

"Andy, you don't look well."

"I'm glad we're not wired for sound," she said lightly, hoping the camera couldn't detect how insincere and shaky her smile was.

"I don't mean in a physical sense," Michael Ratliff continued. "You know I think you're beautiful. You're unhappy about something. Lyon tells me that you're leaving this afternoon."

Out of the corner of her eye she saw Jeff thrashing through the trees as he followed their progress. Trained to know better, she didn't look at the camera he was toting on his shoulder along with the recorder. This stroll through the woods was supposed to appear candid and unrehearsed. The conversation certainly was.

"Did he tell you he ordered us to leave?"

"I don't think he likes this Mr. Trapper."

"I'd say that's an understatement. He doesn't like any of us."

"He likes you." Andy caught herself from stumbling on the pathway just in time. The general went on, unaffected by either her stunned reaction or the camera. "Lyon's been acting strange lately. We rarely see him during the daytime. He's up and out at dawn and usually doesn't come in until dinner. Often not even then. Since you've come, he's been hanging around the house like a pup waiting for kitchen scraps."

"He's only protecting you. He warned me about tiring you, prying into your personal affairs."

"I think that's what's wrong with Lyon. He's been dwelling too much on the state of my life and not enough on his. If you ask me, his is in worse shape than mine."

They had reached the clearing, where Tony and Warren were standing by with Gil, who was hovering over his battery-powered microphones like a mother hen. A chair for Andy was positioned next to the wheelchair. As soon as the mike levels had been checked and the roar of the river water filtered out as well it as could be, Jeff began to record the last interview on video tape.

Tony fell asleep against a tree, since he didn't have lights to worry about. Warren hastily scratched Andy's questions on a tablet. They would be needed when she was ready to do reverse questions. Gil sat cross-legged on the ground, listening to the interview through his headset. Les hunkered down behind Jeff, tapping his thumbnail against his teeth as he listened. Lyon, leaning against a cypress with his ankles and arms crossed, glowered at all of them.

At what point in the interview Andy lost control, she never could pinpoint. One minute she was asking questions about the war, keeping them nonspecific as the general had requested, and the next she was laughing over a story he was telling about a French farmer and his wife who had hidden a whole platoon of GIs in their hayrick.

From there on General Michael Ratliff related story after story. His recital was peppered with "Ike said," and "George decided." Tony awakened from his nap to listen. Soon all of them were laughing. Gil didn't even try to filter the laughter out. Andy even saw Lyon smiling at one of the more colorful stories.

The general was laughing and animated, thoroughly enjoying himself. When Andy got a frantic time cue from Warren, she gracefully deterred the general from embarking on another story and ended the interview.

"Oh, General Ratliff, that was wonderful," Andy said, taking off her mike and handing it to Gil. She leaned over the old man and undid the clip that held his mike and hugged him heartily.

"I got rather carried away, I'm afraid."

"You were priceless."

"What'd you think, Les?" Jeff asked excitedly.

"It was okay."

"I don't even think we need reverse questions," Jeff said.

"I'll leave it up to you," Les said.

"Dad, are you all right?" Lyon came up behind Andy to ask.

"I've not had so much fun in years. Some of those stories I didn't even know I remembered until I started telling them. Imagine me thinking of them after all this time." He chuckled again, lost in his private thoughts. Then his eyes became misty, and he clasped his son's hands. Looking up at Lyon, he said quietly, "It wasn't all bad, Lyon. Now that I think on it, it wasn't."

"We'd better get you back to the house," Lyon said and started the motor on the wheelchair. He walked at its side, a protective hand resting on his father's frail shoulder.

"What do you think he meant by that?" Les asked Andy as they followed the others up the incline.

"Meant by what?"

"Don't go stupid on me, for God's sakes, Andy. What did he mean by 'It wasn't all bad'?"

"Just what he said, I guess. He was telling funny stories. He meant that all his war experiences hadn't been gruesome."

"It was more than that, and you know it," he hissed angrily.

"All I know is that unless you draw blood, you're not happy. Well, I am. I think the interviews went great. If you were looking for some deep, dark secret to come out that would blacken an old man's reputation, then I'm sorry. You'll have to do without this time."

SANDRA BROWN

She marched ahead of him and got to the patio at the same time as the general in his wheelchair did. Lyon was holding the door for him, but the general detained him. "Just a moment, Lyon. I want to speak to Andy. I may not see her again before she leaves."

With her eyes she asked Lyon's permission, and he reluctantly backed away. The cruel lines around his mouth devastated her. She would leave him unforgiven for what he saw as her duplicity.

She knelt beside Michael Ratliff. He took her hand between the two of his and squeezed it hard. "I know you'll think this the wistful daydreaming of an old man, but I had a feeling about you before I ever heard you lurking outside the door that day. You became very real to me that night Lyon ranted and raved about your tenacity, your gall. As angry and uncomplimentary as he was about you, I think his meeting you had a profound effect on him, Andy. I think you were supposed to come into our lives.

"I ask you bluntly. Old men don't have time for tact. Are you in love with my son?"

She laid her head on his bony knee and squeezed her eyes against the tears she could feel welling up in them. She nodded her head, then raised it to look up at him. "Yes, yes, I am."

His wavering hand stroked down from the crown of her head to her cheek. "I hoped as much. I prayed as much. You'll be good for him. Don't fret over the present. Think in terms of the future. If this love you have for him is true, things will work out. I promise."

174

She knew otherwise, but she didn't want to dampen his optimism. She stood up only to lean down and kiss him softly and lingeringly on the cheek. They didn't say good-bye, but stared at each other pensively until Lyon came forward to assist him into the house.

It had been prearranged that the crew would drive the van to the bunkhouse, pack their gear, and then guide Les to the Haven in the Hills as he followed in the car he had rented in San Antonio. Andy would come after them in her rental car as soon as she was packed.

She scanned the room quickly, checking to see if she'd forgotten anything. She wouldn't think about what leaving meant. If she thought about it, she'd die. So she'd wait until later, when she'd have the luxury of wallowing in her misery alone.

Knowing she had postponed her leavetaking too long, she went to the door of the bedroom and opened it. Lyon was standing on the threshold. His face was expressionless. No anger. No victory. No love. As void and empty as she felt on the inside.

"My bags are ready. I was just going down," she said hastily, thinking that he might have come upstairs to boot her out.

He didn't say anything, but backed her into the room and closed the door behind him. She took two more steps backward. "Your father? How is he?"

"Extremely tired. I called the doctor to come out and take a look at him. He's with him now."

"I hope today wasn't too strenuous, but . . ." Her voice trailed off. Why couldn't she think of anything to say? She certainly didn't want to increase Lyon's fury by reminding him that he was the one who had insisted on having the interview this afternoon.

He took a few steps toward her until they were only inches apart. Taking one of her wrists in each of his hands, he pulled her around until her back was to the door. He pinned her hands on either side of her face at shoulder level.

"It looks like you're well on your way to a big network job, Ms. Malone. It's a shame you don't have that earth-shaking story you hoped for. I hate for you to have gone to all the trouble you did and go away empty-handed. Here's something to take with you."

She expected his mouth to be hard and abusive, but it was soft and persuasive. He was using the oldest tactic in the strategist's manual: Placate the enemy, give him misplaced confidence, treat him kindly, and then go in for the kill. Even though she knew what he was up to, she was powerless to defend herself.

Her mouth opened against his like a flower, and he wasted not a motion in taking all of it. He sipped her slowly. His fingers around her wrists relaxed, and his open palms slid over hers. Fingers intertwined and locked.

His tongue delved between pliable, yielding lips. His hips ground against hers as he pressed her into the door. He found a satisfying position and drummed against her with his hips even as his tongue pumped into her mouth.

It was meant to be a debasing and insulting embrace, but somewhere in time it changed character. He was no longer moving against her with contempt, but angling against her with need. The stroking of his body along hers quit its quick, brutal quality and became sustained and sensual. He whispered her name, and it was as if the word had been ripped from his throat.

She whirled in a vortex of emotions, hating him for reducing her to the mindless creature she became at his touch, yet wanting him, craving him, loving him. He absorbed her. All she knew or cared about was Lyon. Lyon Lyon. Lyon.

Just as suddenly as he had seized her, he released her, throwing her from him as if she were something revolting. His breathing was like that of a man who had run a long way. "Now, go tell Les all the details of that. I'm sure he's waiting for a full report."

Mortification and agonizing pain boiled to the surface as consummate rage. "You—" She sucked in air. "You sanctimonious, stubborn fool. You think—"

"Lyon! Lyon!"

They heard the panic in Gracie's voice and rushed out onto the landing to see her puffing up the stairs. "Lyon, Dr. Baker says to come quick. Your father . . ."

Chapter Nine

The wind tore at her hair and dried the tears as soon as they fell from her eyes. She was driving with the window down, praying that nature would find a way of anesthetizing her heartache.

With only a few snatches of clear memory Andy pieced together the confusion and despair of the last hour.

She and Lyon had raced down the stairs. He had gone into his father's bedroom while she comforted a weeping Gracie. The doctor came out of the room, shaking his head sadly in response to their inquiring eyes. After what must have been a half-hour Lyon had come out of the room, dry-eyed but haggard. He didn't look at her. He didn't see anything as he conferred quietly with the doctor. Soon after that the ambulance arrived, and Andy watched with horror as the draped body of General Michael Ratliff was loaded into its sterile confines. Lyon followed it in his car down the winding drive.

She had left Gracie still sad, but setting about to do all the hundreds of things that would have to be done. Lyon would have her support and love. That was good.

Arriving at the motel while the sky was turning a deep indigo, Andy assumed the crew and Les had gone to dinner. She checked into the room they had reserved for her. It was dismally similar to the first one she'd occupied.

She locked her door, took her telephone off the hook, and curled into the bed. For the next eight hours she pretended to sleep.

"General Ratliff, the last surviving five-star general of World War II, had lived in seclusion on his ranch near Kerrville, Texas, since his early retirement in 1946. The general died peacefully at home after a long illness. Private funeral services will be held at the ranch tomorrow."

Andy watched the anchorman on the morning news show as he dispassionately read the story. She wondered when Lyon had officially notified the news services of his father's death.

"The President, after hearing of General Ratliff's death, had this to say."

Andy listened to the President of the United States as he acclaimed the retired general, but the person he spoke about in terms of heroics and medals had no relevance to the old gentleman she knew. Only yesterday she had talked to him of his son and how she loved him. He had taken her hand and held it firmly, pressing it between his two frail ones, telling her with his eyes that he wholeheartedly endorsed her love for Lyon.

"Let me in." Andy jumped when Les pounded on the door.

"Just a . . . minute."

There was no sense in delaying what was to come. She found her robe at the foot of her bed and pulled it on, wishing it were a suit of armor. She went to the door and opened it.

"When did you find out about it?" he demanded without preamble.

"Last evening." There was no redemption in lying. "He died just as I was leaving."

"And you didn't see fit to tell me?" Les roared.

"What good would it have done?"

"What good? Damn, I'd like to shake some sense into you."

She ignored his tantrum. Going over to a chair, she folded herself into it and raised her knees to prop her forehead against them. She was remembering how General Ratliff had looked at her the last time. He had known he was about to die. His good-bye had been a silent one.

"Andy, what the hell is the matter with you?"

When Les's brash, insensitive question had penetrated her mind, she lifted vacant eyes to him. After several seconds his image swam into focus. "Les, a man I admired is dead. How can you possibly ask what the matter is?"

He shifted his eyes toward the curtained window that let in no sunlight. "I know you admired him, but he's still a man who means news, and we're news people. You didn't see that announcer crying just now, did you? Andy, have you thought that we're sitting on a gold mine?"

She shook her head. Les had gone to the window and whisked open the draperies. The sunlight hit her full in the face. She shaded her eyes against it. "What do . . . a gold mine?"

"Think, Andrea, for God's sakes! We've got the only interviews General Ratliff granted since he became a damn hermit. Now he's dead, and we're sitting on hours of tape of him. Do you know what that can mean?"

Lowering her knees and standing up, she walked to the window and looked out onto a gorgeous day. It wouldn't be gorgeous for Lyon. He'd have to arrange a funeral.

"Andy?"

"What?"

"Are you listening?"

She ran a hand through her tangled hair. "You asked if I knew what having the tapes of General Ratliff could mean."

Les cursed under his breath. "Let me spell it out for you, then. You may have been sitting on the knowledge that the old general had croaked for personal reasons, and I'm likely never to forgive you. But I intend to sell those tapes to the network and for a helluva lot more than our first bargaining price. This is our way in, and with or without you I'm going to take it."

"Wait, Les." She held up one hand while rubbing her aching head with the other. Why was he bothering with this now? "They're not even edited yet. No music—"

"What the hell do we care? Let them produce them the way they want to. They want them on their evening newscasts tonight. I've already contacted a producer. He about wet his pants, he was so excited. We're to send the tapes air express to New York pronto. I guess we'll have to drive to San Antonio, so hustle it." His hand was already on the door knob.

"Les, please, slow down and let me think." She went back to the bed and sank onto the mattress. "I never thought of airing the interviews after the general's death. I never intended them to be an obituary."

"I know that." She could tell by Les's grating tone that he was fast losing patience but was trying not to fly off the handle. "That's the way it turned out, Andy. You knew the old, uh, general was going to die soon."

"Soon, yes, but not while I was there to see it." She covered her face with her hands. "It seems so cold somehow, so disrespectful to air them now."

"I can't believe what I'm hearing," Les shouted and slapped his hands against his thighs. "What's happened to you?"

Lyon. Lyon. Lyon had happened to her. And General Michael Ratliff had happened to her. The story she had gone to do had diminished in importance when compared to the men they were. But what about the interviews would be detrimental to the general's memory? Nothing. She had kept them that way. So if she went along with Les on this, he'd leave her alone for a while.

"All right," she said wearily. "Do whatever you have to do. But I'll follow you to San Antonio later. I want to stay here a while."

"You bet you will. I want you to do a follow-up report outside the gates of the ranch. We've got the crew here. The place will be crawling with press by noon, we can get a jump on everybody. While I drive the tapes to San Antonio and put them on a plane, you and the guys can go back out there—"

"No. Absolutely not," she said, slicing the air with her hands. "I'll go along with selling the tapes because I'd like the American people to see the way he was during his last days. But I'll not be a vulture at a funeral."

"Andy, for God—"

"I won't, Les. That's final."

"I wish to hell you'd gone ahead and slept with that cowboy and gotten him out of your system. Maybe then you'd be acting like the Andy Malone I've known all these years. I assure you he's got the same equipment all the rest of us have."

"You're going too far, Les." She stood with her hands clenched at her sides, her posture perfectly erect. The golden eyes gleaming at him were those of a lioness confronting a potential predator of her young. He got the message loud and clear.

"Okay, okay." He went to the door. "I'll send the crew out to shoot some video. Someone else can record a track onto it later. Jeff said you had the interview tapes. Where are they?"

The tapes were labeled and stored in black plastic cases. Andy had them all in a canvas bag. She was holding it out to Les when he asked, "Is the release in there, too?"

Her mind went on a rapid hunt, looking in each corner of her brain for the time and place when she had had General Ratliff sign the permission form that would allow them to air the interviews on television. Such a scene couldn't be found. One hand tightened around the canvas bag while the other came up to cover her mouth. "Oh, Les," she breathed.

"What's wrong?"

"Th—the release form. I never had Michael Ratliff sign one."

She shrank from the murderous cold blue glint in Les's eyes. "You can't mean that, Andy. Try to remember. You've never done an interview in your career that you didn't get the release first. Now, goddammit, where is it?" By the time he reached the last word, he was screaming.

"I don't have it," she yelled back. "I remember that when we started taping, I wanted to hurry before the general got tired. Gil's cord had gone dead, remember? And we'd had to delay. I remember thinking that I'd get it later. I never did."

He slammed his fist into his palm, and she heard words she'd never heard him use before, and she'd thought she'd heard them all. He rounded on her. "You're not lying are you? Is this some ruse—"

"No. I swear it, Les. I never got a release form signed."

"It'd be just like Lyon to sue our asses for all we're worth if we ran them without one. And even if he didn't know he had that power, the network would, and they'd never take the chance. You'll just have to go out there and get him to sign one."

"No."

"What do you mean no?"

"I mean no. Not until after the funeral."

"That's tomorrow," Les shouted.

"That's right. I'll not go out there until then. Lyon may not even let me in."

Les looked at the bag she held in her hand. He was gnawing his lip and flexing his fingers. "Forget taking these tapes by force or faking a release. I'd telephone the network myself and tell them what you were trying to pull."

"It never crossed my mind," he said with a feral smile.

"Yes, it did," she said, not smiling. "Go call your contact and tell him he won't have the interviews until after the funeral. Then leave me alone for the rest of the day."

He stood at her door, hands on hips, looking at her for a long time. He shook his head in wonder. "You've changed, Andy. I can't understand what's happened to you."

"That's right, Les. You can't understand."

The remainder of the day was spent lying on the bed with a cold compress over her eyes. She locked the tapes in her suitcase and hid the key. She also kept the door to her room locked and the chain latched. She swore to herself that she trusted Les, but actions spoke louder than words.

Since she had slept little the night before, she dozed off and on during the day. As she hovered between sleep and wakefulness the scenes that were acted out in her mind fell somewhere between dreams and fantasies. She and Lyon were the featured players in all of them.

In the early evening she watched the accounts of General Ratliff's death on the network news shows. As Les had predicted, the entrance to the ranch was thronged with reporters and photographers. Police barricades had been set up to keep back the throng. Only locals or veterans who had served under the general's command during the war were permitted to parade past the gates. Most of them left sprays of flowers.

Andy's heart constricted when Lyon was shown coming through the gates to deliver a terse statement to the press. To the people who had come to pay their last respects to his father he was seen speaking softly, graciously, solemnly.

He was dressed as Andy had never seen him, in a dark suit and white shirt. His carriage, his control, the strength he exuded were impressive. Her throat ached with emotion. He put up a good front for the public, but what was he suffering in private? *Has Jerri come home to comfort him in his time of need?* Andy wondered. Instantly she regretted her peevishness, though the idea of his finding comfort in another woman's arms continued to haunt her.

The following morning the news programs had little to report about the funeral, except that the President was flying in by helicopter from Lackland Air Force Base to attend the ten o'clock graveside service. The general was to be interred on the ranch.

Andy put on a chamois-colored shirtwaist dress and matching high-heeled sandals. She pulled her hair into a smooth bun and slipped small gold earrings into her ears.

By noon she had packed everything and loaded it in her rental car, planning to leave Kerrville for good as soon as she returned with the signed release and delivered it to Les. The crew, after they had covered the funeral from outside the gates, had gone on to San Antonio in hopes of catching a late-afternoon plane to Nashville. Though none of them spoke of it, Andy knew they had been affected by the general's death.

At three o'clock Les came to her room to see her off. He had argued for her to leave earlier. She had refused.

"When will you be back?" he asked.

"When I get it signed," she said. His irritation made his red hair stand on end. To clarify the ambiguity of this, she said, "I don't know what I'll find when I get out there. The police may still be there. I don't know if I'll get anywhere near the place. I'll be back as quickly as I can."

He was still throwing daggers at her as she wheeled out of her parking space. Her hands were so damp, they slipped on the steering wheel of the car. What she had told Les was true—she didn't know what she'd find when she got to the ranch, but she almost wished she wouldn't be able to get in. She dreaded meeting Lyon face to face much more than facing a police barricade.

There was no barricade, only the same guard who had been at the gate the day she arrived. Hundreds of sprays of flowers were wilting in the summer sun. She drove the small car up to the guardhouse and lowered the window.

"Hello," she said.

"Hidy," the man said. His eyes were red-rimmed and Andy's heart twisted with compassion.

"I'm Mrs. Malone. I was with—"

"Yes, ma'am. I know who you are."

"I was wondering if I might go in for a few minutes."

He took off his hat and scratched his head. "I don't know. Mr. Ratliff said no one was to go in."

"Would you call the house for me? Tell him it's very important that I see him just for a moment."

"I guess I could do that."

He ambled back into the guardhouse, and Andy could see him dialing and then speaking into the telephone.

When he came back out, he was already reaching for the lever that opened the electric gate. "I didn't talk to Mr. Ratliff, but Gracie said it was all right for you to come in."

"Thank you very much." She put the car in gear and drove in. The house and outbuildings were deserted. No ranch hands were evident, as they usually were, going about their chores. Even the cattle grazing on the slopes of the hills seemed abnormally still.

Before she could ring the bell on the front door, it was flung open and Gracie hurled herself at Andy. "God bless you for coming when you did, Andy. I don't know what I would have done with him. He's in his office, and I think he's drinking. He held up so well. Then as soon as everyone left, he went sort of crazy, like. He won't eat and practically threw a tray at me when I took it in to him. If he wasn't so big, I'd whip him good for acting so hateful. You'll go in and talk to him, won't you?"

Andy looked with trepidation at the door to the room she knew was Lyon's office. "I don't think I'd improve his disposition, Gracie. I'm the last person he'd want to see."

"I have my own opinion on that. I think your leaving is the reason he's carrying on so."

Andy turned to her in shock. "He just lost his father."

"And he's been expecting to any day for a year. He feels bad about it, no doubt, but it ain't natural for a man to carry on so. He's sick at heart, and it ain't all because of the general's death." Her bottom lip quivered, and Andy reached out to embrace her.

"I'm sorry, Gracie. I know how you loved him."

"I did. And I'll miss him. But I'm glad he's not feeling bad anymore. Now please go in and see to Lyon. He's the one I'm truly grieving for."

Andy lay her purse and the forgotten release form on the hall table. "You say he's drinking and won't eat?"

"Hasn't had a bite since . . . I can't even remember when."

"Well, first things first. Bring me the tray you fixed him."

Within minutes Gracie was back with a tray laden with cold fried chicken, potato salad, a gelatin salad, and slices of buttered bread. Andy took it from her and carried it to the door. "Open it, please." Gracie did as she was asked and stepped back hurriedly, as if she expected to be fired upon from within.

Andy stepped into the darkened room, and Gracie softly shut the door behind her. The drapes on the wide windows had been drawn to prevent any sunlight from seeping in. The leather furniture, the heavy oak desk, and the overflowing bookcases contributed to the oppressive atmosphere in the room. That and the reek of whiskey coming from the opened bottle on the desk where Lyon's disheveled head lay on his bent arm.

She walked farther into the room, making no effort to muffle her footsteps. When she stepped off the area rug and her heels tapped on the tile, he stirred, then raised his head.

She saw the roar forming on his lips. She also saw it die before it was uttered. Astonishment killed it. He stared at her blankly for a moment, then his bleary eyes focused and he snarled, "What are you doing here?"

Her first impulse was to drop the tray and rush to him, offering her loving condolences. But she knew he would resent that kind of sentimentality and rebuke her for it. She'd have to be tough and meet him head on. "I would think that was obvious. I'm bringing you something to eat."

"I don't want anything. And I especially don't want you, so leave. Now."

"You may have terrorized your housekeeper, but you can't frighten me. I don't scare easy. So why don't you act like a civilized adult and eat this food. Gracie is sick from worrying about you. Personally I don't care if you hole up in here and drink yourself into oblivion, but she does. And I *do* care for her. Where do you want it?" Without waiting for an answer, she clunked the tray down on the desk in front of him.

"I didn't see you with the rest of the bloodsuckers this morning. Oversleep?"

"Insult me if it makes you feel better, Mr. Ratliff. You're very good at insults. Also rudeness, stubbornness, and chauvinism. I didn't know, however, that you were prone to cowardice."

He lurched out of the chair unsteadily and had to brace himself on the edge of the desk. "Cowardice?"

"Yes. You're a coward. You seem to think that you have a monopoly on misery. That you've been singled out to suffer unduly. You don't know the first thing about suffering, Mr. Ratliff. I've talked to a man without any hands or feet. Do you know what he does? He's a marathon runner.

"I've interviewed a woman who was paralyzed by polio from the neck down. Her condition is so bad that she lives on her back in an iron lung that does her breathing for her. She smiled during the whole interview, she was so proud of her artwork. Artwork? Yes! She paints by holding a brush between her teeth."

"Wait a minute! Who appointed you as my conscience?"

"I did."

"Well, save it. I never said that there weren't others far worse off than me." He flopped back into his chair.

"No, but you exult in your martyrdom because your wife left you. You're holding a grudge against the whole world because of her." She propped herself on her arms as she leaned over the desk. "Lyon, grief for your father is justified," she said softly. "But don't lock yourself away in here and let your wounds fester. You're too valuable."

"Valuable?" he asked on a bitter laugh. "Jerri didn't think so. She was unfaithful even before she left."

"So was Robert."

His head snapped up, and his bloodshot eyes looked at her for a long time. Then he dragged his hands down his face, momentarily distorting the ruggedly handsome features, stretching the skin of his face downward like a rubber mask. When it settled back in place, he reached for the liquor bottle. Andy held her breath, then released it slowly when he recapped the bottle and put it in the desk drawer.

Looking boyishly contrite, he said, "Pass the chicken, please."

She relaxed the tension that was holding her shoulders erect and slid the tray over to him. He laughed. "How many is this for?"

"Gracie said you hadn't eaten for a while. She thought you'd be hungry."

"Join me?"

"There's only one plate."

"We can share it."

Gracie nearly upset her cup of coffee as she jumped up from the table in the kitchen when Andy carried in the empty tray.

"How is he?" Gracie asked cautiously.

"Full," Andy laughed. "I ate some, but he demolished every morsel. He'd like something to drink. Not coffee. I think with a little encouragement, I might be able to get him to sleep for a while."

"I'll fix a pitcher of iced tea."

"Yes, that would be good. Gracie,"—she paused before voicing her next request—"I want you to do something for me."

"Anything after what you've done for Lyon."

"Call the Haven in the Hills and leave a message for Mr. Trapper. I don't want you to give it to him, because he's going to be upset and you don't deserve the verbal abuse. The message is that he will get what he's waiting for in the morning."

"He'll get what he's waiting for in the morning."

"Yes." She wasn't going to mention the release to Lyon now. His mood was mellow, and they were communicating on a level they never had before. She didn't intend to do anything that would jeopardize this new trust he had placed in her. "You'd better notify the man at the gate that under no circumstances is he to let anyone else in today."

"Right," Gracie said smartly.

"I think that's everything. With any luck Lyon will be asleep shortly."

"Thank you, Andy. I knew you were just what he needed."

Andy nodded, but she didn't say anything before carrying the tray with the pitcher of tea and two tall glasses into the office. Lyon was no longer seated behind the desk, but sprawled on the leather sofa with his eyes closed. His hands were folded over his belt. He was in shirtsleeves. His vest, coat, and necktie were heaped on a chair.

Andy crept toward him on silent feet. She got to within inches of him before he opened his eyes. "I thought you were asleep."

"Just resting."

"Would you like some iced tea?"

"Yes."

"Do you take sugar?"

"Two." She shuddered. "I take it that means you prefer your tea unsweetened."

"I was remembering that syrup I had to drink at Gabe's. He must use three or four teaspoons in every glass."

"Why did you drink it?"

"I had to do something while I was getting up the courage to speak to you."

"Robert cheated on you?"

The change of subject was so abrupt that Andy's face revealed the same sudden shock as it had when she'd first learned, through a "friend," of her husband's unfaithfulness. "Yes."

Lyon sighed and traced patterns on the frosty glass with his fingertip. "I've taken many women to bed. I think that most of those times were mutually enjoyable. But never while I was married. I demanded absolute fidelity from both of us. I think that's the way a marriage should be."

"You probably learned that from your father. Gracie said that even after your mother died, he had no interest in other women."

"He loved her up until . . . until he died."

That opened the floodgate, and he began talking about his parents, particularly about the father whom he had loved and respected. "It wasn't easy being the son of a living legend. Sometimes I resented that. Everyone expected more of me because of who my father was. His self-imposed exile had an effect on my youth. For instance we never traveled as a family, never went on vacations. When I was older, he let me go on trips with friends and their families."

He talked about the funeral, the flag-draped coffin, the President and his kindness.

"Are you a political proponent of his?" she asked.

"Not at all, but he's an awfully nice man." They laughed and he asked her about the current President's predecessor, whom she had interviewed.

She began telling him how the interview had come about, but after she had gotten a few sentences into her tale, she saw that his eyes were closed and his head was listing to one side as it lay against the back of the sofa. She took the half-full glass out of his hand and set it with her own on the coffee table. Waiting a few minutes until his breathing was deep and even, she put her hands on his shoulders and eased his head down onto her chest as she positioned herself in a reclining position in the corner of the sofa.

He stretched out quite naturally in his sleep to lie beside her. She measured the breaths that struck her skin in moist puffs. Her fingers sifted through his thick dark hair, and it curled around them like silken tentacles. She touched his face, loving it. Her hand smoothed down his broad back.

Once he adjusted his head more comfortably on her breast. The word he murmured might have been her name, but it might have been only her wishful imagination. She held him tight, whispering endearments and expounding on the love she'd never have had the courage to speak of if he were awake. Then she, too, slept.

When she awoke, he was kissing her breasts through the cloth of her dress. His hand stroked down her stomach to find her femininity and cup his hand over it.

"Lyon?" she whispered.

"Andy, please," he groaned, "I want to make love."

Chapter Ten

"I need you. Right or wrong, whether it makes sense or not, I need you, Andy."

Her fingers burrowed in his hair. There was no resistance on her part as the buttons on her dress fell away, nor when her brassiere was undone. He buried his face in the velvet cleft between her lush breasts. He was like a child seeking sustenance as his mouth planted frantic kisses on her flesh.

The man who was usually controlled and adept became clumsy and incompetent as he sought the hemline of her dress. She aided him in ridding her of restrictive undergarments. He grappled with the zipper of his trousers, haste making his movements jerky and desperate.

He came to her without preamble, but her body was ready to receive him. She sheathed him completely and

tightly, taking his pain and sorrow and heartache into herself. With each thrust he emptied himself of bitterness
and callousness. She accepted it. If her body could give
him this comfort, then she wanted to be the remedy for
his spiritual illness. It had nothing to do with sex and
everything to do with love. And when it was over, she
was grateful for the chance to have loved him uncondi-
tionally, giving all, receiving nothing.

Not speaking, not moving, she held him fast while he
rested, his head a beloved burden on her shoulder. She
listened to each breath, cherishing the sound. His heartbeats were absorbed by her breasts, and she gloried in
that steady throbbing.

He raised his head. When he saw the tears rolling from
the corners of her golden eyes into her hair, he was filled
with remorse. "God, Andy, I'm sorry. I'm sorry," he said,
shaking his head. He left her, and the awkward attempts
he made to restore her clothing were endearing. He
cradled her head against his chest and stroked back her
hair.

"I don't know what happened to me. I didn't even kiss
you before . . . What a bastard I am. I made you cry. You
must feel ravished. Raped. God, I'm so sorry," he choked
out.

She lifted her head and held his face between her hands.
"Stop this. Now. I'm crying because I'm glad you needed
me."

"I did. I do. I can't imagine that after the last two days
this would be what I need, what I want."

Her smile was tender as she smoothed the black brows. "You've been obsessed with the thought of death. I think you needed to know you were still alive. To celebrate life."

His eyes were like glowing coals, gray at the edges but smoldering with fire in their centers. "Is it even possible, that with all that's happened between us, the animosity, the anger, the mistrust, that I've fallen in love with you, Andy Malone?"

"I don't know. Is it? I hope so. Because I love you very much, Lyon."

"Andy." Her name was a reverent whisper as his thumbs caressed her lips. Then he chuckled softly. "Andy. I never thought I'd love someone named Andy. Much less think I was going to die if I didn't kiss this Andy."

Then his mouth was open and moving over hers. He made up for the swiftness, the near violence of what had happened moments ago with the gentle leisure of this kiss.

His tongue tasted her lips, licking them softly with its tip. He kissed the corners of her mouth until they quivered with the need to open to him. He pressed inside and swept her mouth. Palate, teeth, the inside of her lips knew the marauding of his tongue. It rubbed against hers and coaxed it into his mouth. The pressure found there was so sweet, she clung to him weakly.

When he took pity and gradually eased away, they both breathed deeply of the essence of the other. He continued his adoration by nibbling her throat, the beginning of a journey the final destination of which was her ear.

"When did you learn to kiss like that?" she asked on a soft moan as his teeth caught her earlobe.

"Just now. Kissing hasn't ever seemed that important until now."

"And it's important now?"

"Very."

"Why?"

"So you'll know how much you're loved."

He kissed her again. This time his mouth was still, taking possession of hers, plunging his tongue deeply and holding it there. His arms held her imprisoned against him, and she felt the stirrings in his loins that were answered in her own.

"Can you forgive me my former selfish insensitivity and come upstairs with me?"

She nodded and they vacated the sofa. Quietly they gathered up discarded clothing, straightened what they were still wearing, and left the office.

It was nighttime, the sun having set long ago, for it was dark out. They paused to listen, but could hear no noise coming from the kitchen or Gracie's room beyond.

"Are you hungry?" he asked politely, and Andy's smile was wide.

"What would you do if I said yes?" she teased.

"Swallow real hard and try to keep from crying."

She took his hand and led him up the stairs. She thought he would take her into his room, but at the door of the bedroom she had occupied he stopped.

"Let's go in here."

"Why?"

"You'll see."

They went into the moonlit room. Neither saw fit to turn on the lights since the room was bathed with a silver phosphorescence.

"Don't move," he instructed as he began to shed his clothes.

Obediently she sat on the edge of the bed where he had set her and watched with delight as first his shirt, then pants and underwear came off. He was such a marvelous specimen of the male animal that she was at once proud enough of him to want to show him to the world and at the same time fiercely jealous of every other woman who had ever seen him this way.

"Come here," he said, extending his hand.

She stood up and went to him. He moved behind her and, settling his hands on her waist, maneuvered her toward the cheval glass that stood in the corner near the windows. She had admired the piece of furniture since the first time she entered the room. It stood almost seven feet tall. Made of rosewood, the oval frame was intricately carved. The frame holding the swivel mirror was sturdy, but gave the impression of delicacy. The piece was no doubt over a hundred years old, but the mirror had been resilvered so that their reflection showed up clearly as Lyon stood her directly in front of it.

Standing behind her, his hands reached over her shoulders to unbutton the dress he had so haphazardly rebuttoned a short time earlier. One by one the buttons fell victim to the dexterity of his fingers. With great care he unbuckled the belt at her waist. Taking a side of the bodice in each of his hands, he slid them upward. The backs of his fingers grazed her breasts and she shivered. Weakening, she leaned against him but didn't close her eyes.

Cool evening air settled on her skin as he drew the dress off her shoulders. The cloth whispered down her arms under his guidance. With the merest touch of his hands it slithered over her hips and dropped unceremoniously to the floor. He leaned down to help her step free of it.

"It couldn't get any more wrinkled," he said with a rueful smile as he straightened up. Then she felt him tense, felt his sudden intake of breath as he stared at her reflection in the mirror.

"I don't care if it wrinkles," she sighed, overcome as he was by the moment and the web of sensuality he was slowly spinning around her, making her captive.

Lovingly his hands wrestled with the pins that held her hair until it tumbled free. He took handfuls of it and carried them to his face. He grew intoxicated with its fragrance and buried his face in the golden strands. He lifted the heavy mane from her neck and kissed her there, using his tongue to caress.

When he raised his head and let her hair fall naturally onto her shoulders, their eyes met in the mirror, and they smiled at each other.

His hands glided from her shoulders down to her breasts. Her bra had been hastily refastened when Lyon had fumbled with her clothing, and now her breasts swelled against the gossamer casing. Lightly, so lightly it was almost a suggestion of a caress, his thumbs brushed the crests. If she had not been watching, she might have thought the airy strokes were a product of her imagination or the whimsical notion of a gentle breeze.

But the tightening response was real. He put his lips to her ear and said with masculine satisfaction, "I told you that day in your motel room that this could be easily dispensed with." The front snap of the bra was released, and he slipped the garment from her arms. It, too, found its way to the floor.

"Beautiful," he murmured.

In the mirror she saw his hands close over her breasts. Her flesh strained through his fingers as he squeezed her gently, ever mindful of not hurting her. Moonlight highlighted the dark centers that attracted the attention of his loving fingers. He circled them slowly, arousingly, until she ached with need for him to touch her. When he did, when his fingers made contact with the distended buds, she felt the touch deep in her womb and cried out his name with the wonder of it all.

"I don't know how long I can do this," he grated. "It's a fantasy I wanted to act out. But, God, you're lovely."

His hands slid down her sides, rippling over her ribs. When they reached the waistband of her half-slip, he leaned forward and nudged her head backward until his mouth met hers. As they kissed she felt his palms smoothing past her waist and knew that the backs of his hands were taking her last garment with them on their gradual descent.

Without breaking free of his embrace, she stepped out of the half-slip, which formed a milky pool at her feet. His desire was hard and urgent against the small of her back, but he restrained himself long enough to drink in the splendor of her nakedness.

Together they looked at their images in the mirror. His hand splayed over her abdomen, pulling her against the demanding manhood. His other hand stroked downward to caress her thighs, to feather past the golden triangle, to make promises with his fingertips.

"You confuse me, Andy Malone. You look like an angel, but you feel like a temptress. The sounds you make deep in your throat when I caress you like this are nothing like a heavenly choir, but the most wanton of songs. Golden and ivory, you appear to be a cold, untouchable idol, yet you melt against my touch. Do I worship you, or love you?"

"Love me. Now. Please, Lyon, now." Turning in his arms and greeting the manifestation of his arousal, she left no room for doubt of the response she wanted from him.

His hands captured her beneath the fullness of her hips and carried her to the bed. He laid her down gently, having promised himself that he would never take her so hurriedly as he had done before. It had cheated them both.

He lay beside her and when she rolled against him, he stayed her by placing his hand on her breast. "There's time," he whispered against her breast before kissing it tightly and then taking the swollen tip into his mouth to be loved. His tongue rolled over her nipple in a massage that made her whimper with longing. He plucked at it with his lips and soothed it again with his tongue.

"Please, Lyon."

"I'll never be selfish with you again. Let me love you."

His hands wandered at will. His mouth kissed randomly. Yet he touched her as though each erogenous spot had been mapped out for him. His lips discovered the sensitized skin on the undersides of her upper arms, then traveled down her chest to her breasts, and over her stomach. A nimble tongue ravished her navel and made it his. Then chin, nose, and mouth nuzzled her so intimately that she wept at the sheer pleasure and pain of loving him.

Time and again he brought her to the brink of insensibility, but always kept her poised over it, never letting her fall without him. Then when they both were quaking with need, he covered her and buried himself in the sweet haven of her body.

He rocked her gently, lifting her hips with the palms of his hands so she would know all of him. The fit of their bodies was so precise and the rhythm of their movements so synchronized that later they would marvel over it.

Chanting loving words of praise and adoration, he carried her with him into the sublime.

". . . feels so good when . . ."

". . . deep inside . . ."

". . . yes . . ."

". . . thought you might be lying when you said . . ."

"No, there's been no one since Robert."

"Les?"

"Never, Lyon. I swear it."

"Ah, Andy, it is so good."

"For me, too. And, Lyon, it's never been like this before."

"You mean . . ?"

"Yes. Never before."

"Kiss me."

"Is it too hot?"

"No."

"Too cold?"

"Just right. Where's the soap?" she asked.

"I get to go first," he said.

"No, I do."

Lathered hands worked over a hairy chest. A dainty tongue dared to be adventurous. Fingers idled at his waist.

"Andy?"

"Yes?"

"What's wrong?"

"I'm afraid."

"To touch me? Don't be. Touch me, Andy."

Tentatively she sought him. Bravely she touched him. Innocently she loved him.

"Oh, God, Andy." He covered her hand with his own. "Sweet, sweet love, yes. Yes!" He backed her to the wet tile wall.

"It's your turn now," she said breathlessly.

"I forfeit my turn."

Replete, they lay in bed, an interlocking puzzle of arms and legs. He lazily trailed his fingertips up and down her back as she nestled her nose in his chest hair.

"What did you think of my father, Andy?"

"Why do you ask that now?"

She could feel his shrug. "I don't know. I guess because he was always worried about what people would think of him, how the history books would read."

"He was a great man, Lyon. The more I read about him, the more I admire him as a soldier. But I don't think that's what I'll remember about him. I'll always think of him as kind old gentleman who loved his son, who yearned for the wife long gone, who respected other people, who valued his privacy. Am I right?"

"More than you know." He disengaged himself to scoot up until his back was resting against the headboard. Indifferent to his nakedness, he raised one knee as he pulled her up with him and cradled her against his side.

"Les was right, you know," he said quietly.

She lifted her head to look into his solemn face. "About what, Lyon?" She didn't want to know, but she had to ask because he wanted to tell her.

"About there being a definite reason why my father went into seclusion, about there being a secret behind General Michael Ratliff's withdrawal from both the Army and society."

She lay still, barely breathing.

"He came home a hero, you see, but he didn't feel like one. Have you ever heard of the battle along the banks of the Aisne?"

"Yes. It was a major Allied victory in your father's sector. Thousands of the enemy were killed."

"Thousands of American soldiers, too."

"Regrettably that's the price of victory."

"In my father's eyes it was too high a price to pay."

"What do you mean?"

Lyon sighed and shifted his weight. "He made a costly error in judgment and sent an entire regiment into a virtual slaughterhouse. It happens frequently. Officers risk their troops' lives for the sake of a promotion. Not my father. He valued the life of every man under his command, from his officers to the humblest fresh recruit. When he realized what had happened, he was devastated. He couldn't ever forget that his error had cost the lives of so many men, created so many widows and orphans . . ." his voice trailed off.

"But, Lyon, measured against his valor, one mistake is forgiveable."

"To us, yes. Not to him. He was sickened that the battle was hailed as one of the turning points of the war. He was decorated for it. It was considered a great victory, but it defeated him as a soldier, as a man.

"When he came home and was hailed a hero, he couldn't stand the conflict within himself. He didn't feel like a hero. He felt like a traitor."

"That can't be!"

"Not a traitor to his country, but to the men who had trusted his judgment and leadership. It was a conflict he never could reconcile, so he retired from the Army and came here and shut out the world and all reminders of the lie he was living."

They were quiet for a moment before she said, "No one would have thrown stones at him, Lyon. He was a respected man, a hero, a leader at a time in history when America needed heroes and leaders. It was a battleground that spread out for miles. Amidst all the chaos he may have thought he made a mistake when actually he didn't"

"I know that, Andy, and you know that, but since the time I was old enough to understand his reclusiveness, I was never able to convince him of it," he said sadly. "He died still regretting that one day in his life as though he had lived no other. It didn't matter what the public would have thought if they had known. He judged himself more severely than anyone else could have."

"How tragic for him. He was such a lovely man, Lyon. Such a lovely man."

"He thought highly of you, too," he said on a lighter note and combed through her hair.

She tilted her head back to look at him. "He did?"

"Yes, he told me you had a very nice figure."

"Like father, like son."

"And," he continued, ignoring her barb, "he told me the day he died that if I was so big a damn fool to let you leave, then I deserved to lose you."

"To which you said . . .?"

"It doesn't bear repeating. Suffice it to say, I wasn't in an amenable mood."

"And now?"

"Now, I'm exhausted and want to go to sleep, but can't bear the thought of wasting time sleeping while you're naked in my bed."

"Would it make you feel any better to know that I'm sleepy, too?"

He grinned and kissed her. Lying down, he pulled her back against his chest and snuggled close, adjusting her body to the length of his.

She cleared her throat loudly. "Mr. Ratliff, perhaps you don't realize where your hand is."

"Yes, I do, but I was hoping you wouldn't notice."

"Are you going to be a gentleman and remove it?"

"No. I'm already asleep."

Sunlight made her squint as she was putting on her earrings in front of the cheval glass the next morning. Her image in the mirror reminded her of the night before, when Lyon had admitted her into his erotic fantasy. Her hand trembled slightly, and she didn't recognize the rapturous expression on her face. It had never been there before.

Last night could have been a dream, were it not for the vivid reminders left on her body. Her breasts were lightly chafed by the abrasions of Lyon's whisker-rough cheeks. The nipples tingled with memory of his lips and tongue. There was a heavy sensation between her thighs each time she recalled the way Lyon's body had coupled with hers.

She basked most of all in the luxury of loving and knowing that her love was returned. Each time their loving was made complete, it was more than a physiological blending, but a fusing of spirits as well. His sexual prowess had brought her womanhood to life, a life she had never known was there to discover. But that was only one reason why she loved him. She loved the man, his vulnerability when she had seen him grief-stricken, his strength, his humor. She even loved the temper she had seen unleashed on a few occasions.

Lyon. She loved Lyon.

Soon after they awakened, he had excused himself so they could both dress. He had brought the suitcase from her car before he went to his own room.

As she dressed she planned how she would ask him to sign the release form and tell him of the decision she had made just before falling asleep in his arms. She didn't know what their future held. It hadn't been discussed. Last night they had lived only for the present. But whatever happened between them—and she couldn't imagine a future without him now—she knew her life had to change direction. It couldn't go on as it had. Until she had made that decision, she didn't know how cramped and confined she'd felt. Now she felt free, unchained.

She heard his steps on the stairs and attributed his haste to the same impulse that made her heartbeat quicken with the knowledge that he was near. Making one last hasty inspection of herself in the mirror, she whirled around to greet him as he came through the door.

"At last! My lover returns—" Her words died in her throat as she took in his murderous expression. His eyes fairly sparked with fury. His mouth was thinly twisted into a bitter sneer.

"You lying, scheming—"

"Lyon," she shouted, breaking off the hateful epithet. "What's happened?"

"I'll tell you what's happened. A little slut by the name of Andy Malone has duped me again."

"Duped—"

"Spare me the act, okay," he yelled. "I know now what you're here for."

"Lyon," she said, collapsing onto the bed and staring up at him with bewilderment. "I don't know what you're talking about."

"You don't, huh?" He stalked to the window and looked out, surveying the hills that shone in the morning sunlight. "Okay, I'll play along. Tell me why you came out here yesterday."

"I wanted to see you." That was the truth. Les had provided her with an excuse to return to the ranch, but had it not been for the release, she would have contrived another reason to see him one more time.

"You wanted to see me," he repeated ironically, turning around to bear down on her again. "Touching. No doubt you wanted to comfort me in my bereavement."

"Yes," she wailed, hating the scornful tone in his voice.

"No other reason?" he asked silkily.

"Well, yes. I needed to . . . there was a . . . this . . ."

"Tell me, damn you!" he roared.

She flew off the bed, facing him courageously. "I needed to get your signature on a release form so the interviews with your father could be telecast. There! Is that what you wanted to hear?"

"And you found me soppy drunk and distraught and depressed, and I appealed to your maternal instincts and out of the goodness of your heart you decided to stay and nurse me back to being a whole man again."

"No," she said, shaking her head. "One had nothing to do with the other. I forgot about the release. I only wanted to help you."

"Oh, yeah. Sure you did. And while you were at it, while you were giving me every comfort of your body, with not even the pretense of being demure I might add, you found out what you wanted to know in the first place."

Her cheeks flushed hotly with his scathing insult and her nails cut into her palms. She dare not lose what control was left her. One of them had to remain sane, for surely Lyon had gone mad. "And what was that, Lyon? What was it that I'd sell my body to get? Tell me."

"Your goddamn big story," he said, though his lips barely moved. "I just saw the morning newscast from New York. The announcer is titillating his audience with what's to come on this evening's news. A breakthrough in the story of General Michael Ratliff. Interviews never seen before, taped as recently as the day he died. And who's bringing the world this scintillating account? None other than my bed warmer, and God knows who else's, Andy Malone."

Livid with anger, he strode toward her. "And now you'll really have something to tell them. Dig through the history books today and bone up on the Battle of the Aisne, because you'll want to know all the facts before you tell what really happened."

Like a balloon losing air, she slowly sank back onto the bed. She stared into the face looming above her, trying to identify it as the one that had shared her pillow. Was this mouth that spat such ugly accusations the same one that had whispered poetic words as they languished in the aftermath of love?

"I came here to get you to sign the release," she said without inflection. "Les was negotiating the sale of the tapes with the network. I wanted the country to see those interviews, Lyon. I wanted the people to know your father, whom I loved, the way he was before he died. But that's all. I never intended to tell anyone what you told me in confidence."

"Didn't you? Gracie said that last evening you instructed her to call Les at the motel and leave the message that he would get what he wanted in the morning."

Words so innocently spoken were now hurled back with the impetus of poison darts. "I was referring to the release. The sale couldn't be made until I had obtained that. Les was furious when I realized I didn't have it. He was pressuring me to come out here, but I wouldn't until after the funeral."

"Decent of you."

"You don't believe me," she said in an awesomely low voice. Then growing angry that he could suspect her so readily after last night, she began to speak louder. "Can you reasonably think I planned for you to give me the story about your father last night?"

"Considering my mood, I think you saw me as gullible and talkative. You may not have known what I'd say, but you were sure willing to give it one more try. Well, congratulations. You got more than you bargained for. Your interviews will be worth twice as much now. Be a real boost to your career. So get out of my house and run to Les with your story."

"You bet I'll get out of your house, but not for the reason you think. I don't want to spend a moment longer with a man who has no idea of what being a man is about. Your father could have told you. He had compassion, understanding, forgiveness. You once accused me of being a shell of a woman lacking in human emotions. Look at yourself, Lyon."

He opened his mouth to dispute this, but she rushed on. "You say you resented your father's self-imposed banishment, couldn't understand it. But these walls that kept him shut off from the rest of the world are nothing compared to the walls you've erected around your heart. Your prison is far more confining than his.

"Here," she opened her suitcase and took out the canvas carrying bag. "Here are the bloody tapes. Burn them, toss them in your precious river, or shove them someplace

217

most appropriate. I don't care. I never want to see them again." She flung the case at his feet. "I hope you find happiness with them."

Even after securing her suitcase and grabbing her purse, she was out the door within seconds.

Chapter Eleven

❧

L es Trapper was known for a temper that matched his flame-colored hair. Never, if it could be avoided, did anyone cross him. His blue eyes had the power to freeze and his tongue the power to scorch. Only a fool or a martyr would deliberately provoke him.

Andy felt like neither. She felt nothing, only a desolate detachment as she calmly said, "I left the tapes at the ranch with Lyon. If you want, you can make arrangements with him to get them back, but I'm out of it. He may have destroyed them. I don't know. I don't care."

"Are you telling me," Les ground out between his teeth, "that you left all those hours of valuable tape with that cowboy?"

"Yes, I left them with Lyon." She had dreaded this encounter, but now that it was upon her, she was rather enjoying it. She had driven straight from the ranch to the Haven in the Hills, where she knew Les would be impatiently awaiting her return with the tapes and the signed release.

"Have you gone stark staring crazy?" he shouted. "You're throwing away what's just beyond our grasp, Andy. We've waited for this opportunity for years. Worked for it. What in the hell has gotten into you?" He laughed harshly. "Or do I *know* what's gotten into you? Lyon Ratliff."

"Save your crude one liners for someone who will appreciate them."

"I haven't even begun to get crude. I want those tapes, dammit. You may want to throw away your chance, but I won't let you throw away mine."

"Then you can get them from Lyon."

"You run out on me like this and I'll fire you so fast your head will swim."

"I wasn't intending to come back to work." The stunned expression on his face was gratifying. So, Les was mostly hot air after all. She had called his bluff, and it had worked. "At least not back to Telex."

"What are you talking about? You'll die without that television camera."

"Will I? I don't think so."

"I know so. It's in your blood, Andy. You're good. The best. And you love it. It's your life."

"No, Les," she said loudly. "It's *your* life. I want more out of mine." She wanted to go to this man who had been her friend. To take hold of his shoulders. To shake him. To make him understand. But she knew that was impossible. He'd never understand. "Thank you for the compliment. I know I have the talent, but I don't have the drive." She clutched her fist in front of her stomach. "I don't want to reach the top of the heap by sacrificing everything else.

"My father decided, Robert decided, you decided that this is what I wanted for myself. No one consulted me. I've loved what I've done, but it's all I've got. I have nothing more. I'm thirty now. In ten years I'll be forty, and I may be no further along in my career or I may be the sweetheart of the network, but that's still all I'll have. And eventually someone younger, and prettier, and more talented will come along to replace me, and then where will I be? Left with what? Forgive me, Les, for letting you down, but I want out. A rest. My own life."

"That all sounds real pretty, but it's crap and you know it. You've just fallen hard for a guy and you're wanting to protect him. What happened out there this morning? Did he kick you out?"

"Yes, because he saw the announcement about the interviews being shown on the network news tonight."

"So? Why was he so bent out of shape? He knew the interviews were being sold to the network. In any case, they would have been televised sometime. Why—" He cocked his head to one side and the lid of one eye lowered as he studied her nervous fidgeting. "Wait a minute. You found out something. Didn't you?" When she didn't answer, he encircled her arm with bruising fingers and brought his face to within an inch of hers. "Didn't you?"

She stared up at him fearlessly. He didn't have the power to intimidate or humiliate or hurt her now. All her feelings were lying at Lyon's feet, just as the tapes were. She couldn't be hurt any more. Nor did she see any point in gloating over a secret that would go with her to her grave. Les couldn't be any angrier. He had been her friend for a long time. Looking at it from his point of view, she could see how he would consider this a betrayal.

"No," she said calmly, and looked pointedly at the hand that was squeezing the life from her arm. Slowly it relaxed and then fell away. She looked back up at him. "No, Les. There never was any big secret. Maybe that's why I got so turned off by this project. You go for the jugular. I don't. You see people as potential stories to further your own career. I was coming to think in those terms too, and didn't like myself for it. Now, I see people as human beings, with human frailties and the right to keep those frailties private."

She raised on tiptoes to kiss him on the cheek. "I love you. You've been a good friend. I hope you continue to be. But I don't want to see you for a while. Good-bye."

She went out of the room and to her rental car. She had already started the engine when he came to the door. "Andy," he called, "where are you going?" There was a defeated aspect about him that she'd never seen before.

It tugged at her heart, but she'd made her decision and she was going to stick by it.

When she answered, it was in an unstable, gravelly voice. "I don't know."

She went first to San Antonio and checked into the Palacio del Rio located on the city's famous Riverwalk. At the check-in desk she picked up several travel brochures. A week spent in anonymity sounded wonderful. She'd go somewhere and lie on the beach, eat rich food, and be extremely lazy until she felt like coming home and picking up the pieces of her life and rebuilding them. Mexico? The Caribbean?

What did it matter?

In the long run she would still be alone. Not only had she lost Lyon, she had lost her friend and her job. Never in her life had she been at such loose ends. Somewhere she had read that one's character didn't grow in times of stability, but in times of adversity. If that were so, she should have a character a mile high.

Shaking off the desire to lie in solitary confinement in her hotel room, she forced herself to dress in a cool cotton dress and repair her makeup. She left the hotel on the river side and strolled down the Riverwalk, finally choosing a sidewalk café in which to eat a lonely dinner.

She was admired by many who passed her table, especially men, but she averted her eyes in a way that said a silent, but irrevocable "no" to anything they might have had in mind. Some who walked by her stared, trying to place her. She was accustomed to that. People sometimes recognized her immediately. Others would look at her with perplexity, trying to decide where they knew her from. She often wondered when realization struck them. Maybe not until they saw her again on television. Then they would smack their forehead and exclaim, "Of course, Andy Malone! That's who that was."

She toyed with her salad, but only ate the slices of cantaloupe. The cheeseburger she'd ordered was thick and juicy, but it reminded her of the cheeseburger basket Lyon had ordered at Gabe's, and she could barely swallow the first large bite she took. Besides it wasn't cooked enough to suit her. Or at least that's what she gave herself as an excuse for leaving it virtually untouched on her plate.

Having taken up the time necessary to eat dinner, though she really hadn't eaten it, she wandered down the Riverwalk, which was thronged with conventioneers and tourists. How would she fill up the long hours of the evening?

She paused to listen to the mariachi band. She bought an ice-cream cone and immediately threw it into the nearest trash can. She paused in the doorway of a gallery, but lacked the interest or energy to go in and examine the artwork on display.

One of the barges that carried forty or so tourists on a half-hour excursion down the river was boarding at the dock. She purchased a ticket and was helped aboard by a youth dressed in bleached muslin with a bright Mexican belt wrapped around his waist.

"Go all the way to the front, please," he said in a bored monotone.

She sat on the hard wooden bench and stared out over the water of the San Antonio River. Colored lights, discreetly positioned in the lush foliage bordering the Riverwalk, reflected wavering ribbons on the surface. She paid no attention to the other boarding passengers other than to the little girl, about two years old with blond pigtails, who sat next to her.

Andy smiled at the child's young mother and father. She was fresh and pretty. He had a camera hanging around his neck. A young, attractive family out for an excursion. The poignancy of it was painful.

She turned slightly when she heard the revving of the barge's motor, then did a double take when she saw the last passenger who stepped aboard.

Her heart slammed against her ribs and she whipped her head around to stare unseeingly at the water. She heard the muttered objections as he stepped over other people to get to the front of the launch.

"Sir, sir, there's no more room up front," the young man said. "Would you please take a seat back here?"

"I'm not a very good sailor. I'd hate to throw up on anybody," the low-timbred, hoarse voice said. Andy heard the rustling of clothes and the scurrying of feet as everyone made room for the rude passenger who insisted on sitting at the front of the barge.

The young pilot sounded aggravated as he began his spiel in a monosyllabic drone. The barge pulled away from the dock. A cool breeze taunted Andy's hot cheeks as the boat chugged through the water. The river was shrouded overhead with the mammoth branches of oak and pecan.

"On your left you see the amphitheater where—"

"Hi," Lyon said softly. Only the people sitting close to him were distracted from the tour guide's monologue. "Hi," he repeated, when Andy kept her head resolutely turned away from him.

Finally she looked around. He was sitting across the narrow aisle, wedged between three ladies from the senior citizens group and a pair of airmen from the Air Force base. "Hello," she said frostily and turned back around.

"The trees are said to be older than the Alamo—"

"Excuse me, but are you with anyone?" Her mouth was hanging slack with incredulity as she looked back at him. He turned to the blue-haired ladies, who were eyeing him warily. He dismissed that possibility. "Do you know this lady?" he asked of the little girl. She shook her head, and her mother put her arm protectively around her shoulders. Looking at the two airmen, who were staring at him with admiration, he asked, "Is she with either of you?"

"No, sir," they chorused.

"Good," he said, grinning at them. "I wouldn't want to horn in on anybody else's territory."

Andy looked around her in dismay to see that several more people had turned their attention from the scenic panorama along the river to watch the entertaining show

226

Lyon was putting on. She glared at him. He seemed undaunted.

"She's a great looking chick, isn't she?" he asked of the airmen.

They looked at Andy, then back to Lyon, nodding their heads.

"You are insane," she said under her breath. The three blue-haired ladies were staring first at Lyon and then at her, censure and righteous indignation thinning their lips into pursed disapproval.

"What's a woman with a figure like that doing all alone?" Lyon asked the airmen. "Don't you think she has a terrific figure?"

The airmen assessed her with lustful eyes. Self-consciously she crossed her arms. "I noticed it right off," one of them said to Lyon. His raven-black brow crooked in what could be the beginning of a scowl, but he caught it just in time.

He turned back to Andy. "So did I." Now he was speaking only to her, a new confidentiality in his voice. His gray eyes toured her face. "I think she's beautiful, but I don't think she knows how I feel about her."

"Boo-ful lady," the little girl chirped and patted Andy's knee with a sticky hand.

"Will you spend the night with me, beautiful lady?" Lyon asked softly, looking straight into her wide, golden, mystified eyes.

"Harry . . .?" the mother said worriedly.

"Ignore him," the father said.

"Right on," the first airman said.

"Way to go, buddy," said the second.

The three elderly ladies were rendered speechless.

The tour guide had given up trying to interest his passengers in the sites of San Antonio while there was such drama aboard. All heads were turned to the front of the barge.

Andy stood up in the narrow aisle in a futile attempt to escape. Lyon stood up with her. Mere inches separated them. "Why are you doing this?" she demanded in a loud whisper.

"I want you in my life, Andy. If it means buying a television station or setting one up on the ranch, or whatever it takes to get you to stay with me, I'll do it."

"Why? Why, now, do you want me to stay?"

"Because I love you."

"You said that last night, but this morning you were ready to murder me when you thought I'd tell someone about your father."

"Harry . . .?" the mother said again with rising panic.

"Look at the duckies," the father said to his daughter, who was intrigued by this scene, which was better than anything she'd seen on television.

"It was conditioned reflex, Andy. I didn't trust women after what Jerri did. I didn't like women any more. I'd use them, yes, but not like them. Can you imagine the kick in the gut it was for me to realize I loved you? Gracie was all too eager to point out my stupidity."

"I wonder who Jerry and Gracie are?" asked one of the airmen.

"Shhh," said one of the blue-haired ladies.

"Is Jerry a guy or a girl?" whispered the other airman to his friend.

"I'm not sure I want to know. He said he didn't like women anymore."

"What do you mean?" Andy asked tremulously.

"That you wouldn't have left the tapes with me if you'd ever intended to harm my father. That you didn't lie to me about wanting a simple story about his life just before his death. That it was Les I should be angry with and not you."

"Les?" the mother asked. "I thought his name was Jerry."

"Shhh," said the father.

"I quit my job today, Lyon."

He reached out and took her hand. His thumb massaged the palm. "Why?"

"I could never be objective about the story after I met you. My heart wasn't in it, and Les knew it. I tried to deny it, but he was right." She sighed. "You and your father came to mean more to me than any story."

"Since you quit, what were you going to do?"

She shrugged. "I thought I'd go to Mexico somewhere and lie on the beach until I'd sorted it all out."

"I like Mexico and the beach," he said quietly. He kissed the palm of her hand then lay it against his cheek.

"You do?" she asked in a thin voice.

"Perfect place for a honeymoon."

"I see the moon," the little girl chimed.

"Honeymoon?" Andy parroted.

"And the moon sees me."

"Will you marry me, Andy?"

"Marry you?"

"Can't you hear the man, young woman? He's asked you to marry him. Now answer him so we can all get off this boat."

Andy stared at the elderly lady who had issued the order. Then she surveyed all the eager faces that were staring at her and Lyon. She looked into his expectant face and smiled. "Yes."

"You are a beast," she murmured against the warm skin of his shoulder. "I'm almost afraid to go out in public with you."

"Why is that?" He stretched beside her, his long legs tangling with hers.

"Every time we're in public, you embarrass me. First in Gabe's when you told me to take a certain part of my anatomy back to Nashville and—"

"A delectable part of your anatomy, I might add," he said, patting the smooth curve of her hips.

"Then that night on the river in front of all those—"

"Drunkards."

"And now tonight. Whatever possessed you to propose like that?"

"There's safety in numbers. I was afraid you'd turn me down if I asked you nicely."

"I should have slapped your face."

"But you didn't. I think deep down you have the soul of a hussy." Before she could offer a rejoinder, he was kissing her mouth with a fervor that threatened to give proof to his words.

She curled against him, thrilling to the touch of his naked flesh along her body. A small laugh starting in her chest gained force until it broke through her lips. "I was just thinking about what Gabe Sanders said about you."

"And?"

"He said you were likely to do what you damn well pleased."

"Did he now?" he drawled, tilting her lips up for another long, deep kiss.

They had returned to her hotel room as soon as they could push their way through the curious crowd that disembarked from the barge. The moment he closed the door behind them, he caught her in his arms and said gravely, "Andy, I love you. Don't ever leave me. Marry me."

"I love you, too, Lyon. I want so badly to marry you."

"Children?"

"A man once told me that it was a dreadful waste that I hadn't had children before."

He smiled, his eyes loving her face as it was turned up to his. He cupped it between his palms. "I love the woman you are."

"Less than a week ago you didn't think I was too much of a woman."

"I thought so all along. I just didn't want you to know I did. You scared hell out of me."

"Scared you? How?"

"Because I was so sure about everything. I thought I had my life just the way I wanted it, set apart from everyone. I wanted no commitments and no responsibilities. I certainly didn't want anyone to love me, because that would mean loving her back, and I didn't want to take the risk."

His finger ironed out the crease of her worried frown. "You came along and knocked the slats out from under me. I wanted you from the first time I saw you. Carnal lust. Pure and simple. Then when I saw how you were with Dad and how vulnerable you looked that day we got caught in the rain, I started loving you. I wanted to hate you for reducing me to such a lowly state. But I couldn't. When I had finally driven you away for good, I came to my senses. I had to come after you, praying that you'd have me."

"I'll have you. Now and always," she said with trembling lips. "I had given up hope of having a life with a man I loved. My first marriage was such a disappointment. I was convinced I was cut out for a career, not a home, family. I want to share your life, Lyon, be your partner in everything."

"I meant what I said earlier about a television station. If you want to continue working, that's okay with me."

"I'll think about it on a part-time basis. I may miss it after a while."

"You're too good at it to give it up completely. For all my implications to the contrary, I do recognize your professionalism, your talent."

"Thank you for saying so. But I hope you never stop thinking of me as a sex object."

"You can count on that."

The wide, cool bed received them, and now, an hour later, they were still rejoicing in their professions of love.

"How did you find me?" she asked lazily.

"I called Telex and asked for your next of kin. They gave me your mother's telephone number. I called, introduced myself charmingly and told her I was her future son-in-law, but that I'd misplaced my bride. She was the happy bearer of the news that you had called her from here and that you were planning a trip to Mexico and that I'd better hurry if I intended to catch you in time. I think, Ms. Malone, that she wants to marry you off."

"I guess that long-distance call to my mother this afternoon was worth every penny . . . Oh, Lyon . . . you have such a talent for changing the . . . the subject."

His hand had been lovingly, playfully caressing her breast, plumping it in his hand. A mischievous thumb skated over the dusky nipple, and he watched with a mixture of wonder and delight when it peaked with arousal. It was a temptation not to be denied. He touched it with his tongue.

"You taste so good," he said. The sudden greediness that seized him told her more than did his words. She was drawn into the sweet, wet vise of his mouth.

She arched against him. "Lyon—"

The telephone rang. His vicious curse bounced off the walls. She reached for the phone.

"Don't answer."

"I have to, Lyon. I can't let a telephone ring."

He groaned, but didn't stop her from bringing the telephone to her ear. "Hello."

"Hi, sweet baby, whacha doin'?"

"Les!" she exclaimed. She was too shocked by the sound of the last voice she expected to hear to notice that Lyon didn't seemed surprised by the identity of the caller. Nor did his mouth stop its meandering caress across her stomach. "What . . . how . . . why are you calling?"

"Haven't I always told you never to answer a question with another question? You didn't learn one damn thing in all those years. Anyway"—he sighed resignedly—"I couldn't reach Lyon, so I tracked you down to give him a message. Somehow I get the feeling you'll be seeing him soon."

She glanced down at Lyon's dark head, which was making steady progress down her chest and taking love bites all along the route. "What mess—" She cleared her throat. Lyon was nibbling at a rib. "What message?"

"Tell him that was a helluva generous thing he did to send those tapes to the network. He forged my name on the covering letter, but I forgive him. Those tapes landed me a job! I'll be in my new office overlooking sooty ol' New York in two weeks, baby."

"He did that?" she asked on a high note. She tangled her fingers in Lyon's hair and tried to lever his head off her stomach, but despite the pain she must be causing, he refused to comply. "What was in this . . . ahhh . . . Ly . . . forged covering letter?"

"What was that, Andy? Say, are you all right? You sound kinda weird."

"No, I'm fine," she gasped out. An ardent mouth had returned to her breast. "The covering letter . . .?"

"Oh, it said that regrettably you weren't available, that you were leaving the business for a while to get married, but that I would consider a post as an assistant producer for their evening news show. By God, they hired me!"

"That's wonderful, Les. Oh, L-Lyon . . . that's wonderful." The telephone receiver fell from her hand. Lyon picked it up.

"Andy, Andy? What's going on? Are you—"

"Congratulations on your new job, Les. Andy can't talk anymore right now. She's busy writhing in ecstasy. She'll call you back—in a year or two."